"I'm not going to marry you, Owen."

From somewhere Lallie found some dignity. "Not in three weeks, three years, or thirty. Don't be more of a fool than you already are. It would never work, and you know it."

"I'm not a fool, my girl, and it will work." He was supremely confident.

Lallie stared mutinously across the kitchen at him. "You can't make me," she pointed out.

"I can make you do anything I want. You've gone your own road for the past eight years. Now you'll go mine for a while." A grim smile began to play about his mouth. "You can make it hard or easy for yourself as you choose, Lallie, but that's the way it's going to be!"

The Road to Forever

Jeneth Murrey

Harlequin Books

TORONTO • NEW YORK • LONDON
AMSTERDAM • PARIS • SYDNEY • HAMBURG
STOCKHOLM • ATHENS • TOKYO • MILAN

Original hardcover edition published in 1983
by Mills & Boon Limited

ISBN 0-373-02637-4

Harlequin Romance first edition August 1984

CHAPTER ONE

ALISON Moncke closed the front door of the narrow, three-storied Victorian house behind her and started to climb the two flights of stairs to her small flat on the top floor. She went at it slowly; the stairs, like the house, were narrow and steep, and besides, she felt depressed. The weather was bad—a cold, sharp wind was blowing rain in gusts along the pavement and her boots, fashion boots with thin soles and high heels, didn't keep the wet out—her feet felt damp and cold. She raised a hand to pat her plaited coronet of black hair and sighed. That was wet as well, as were her mac and her umbrella.

Two steps down from the top of the second flight, where the naked light bulb overhead gave a little more light, she hunted through her shoulder bag for her key, knowing that as usual she hadn't put it in the pocket specially constructed to hold it and that it would be right at the bottom of the main compartment, mixed up with the hundred and one other things which had somehow found their way there.

After a scrabble among loose coppers, individually wrapped mints, some spilled Paracetamol tablets and a few ballpoint pens, her fingers closed on the key and she raised her head. The lamp bulb cast a lot of shadows, and she watched a deeper shadow detach itself from the corner by her door to come and stand at the head of the stairs. The overhead light

5

shone on a tall, well built figure dressed in casual, country type clothes, it illuminated thick, russet brown hair and turned the features of the man's face into a grotesque devil's mask where the high cheek-bones and masterful nose cast a black shadow which concealed his mouth and chin.

'Hello, Lallie— aren't you a bit late, or does it always take you an hour and a half to get here from your office?'

The nickname, one she had given herself when her little tongue couldn't manage 'Alison', made her face whiten and her long, gold-flecked grey eyes harden. Nobody in London knew about that nickname, not now—she hadn't used it in the last five years or so and she had hoped never to hear it again, but here was Owen using it as though nothing had ever happened, as though it was nearly six years ago and all the bitter, angry words had never been said.

Her fingers closed convulsively over the key and she drew a deep breath to steady herself before she climbed the remaining two stairs and raised her head to look up at him. She wasn't a big girl and it seemed a long way to look up, her head hardly came to his shoulder, even in high heels. She stood quite still and silent until she judged her voice would be normal.

'Hello, Owen. What are you doing here?'

'Waiting for you, what else?' He stretched out a hand for the key. 'Let me.'

'No, thank you.' Her voice was as colourless as her face and her fingers clutched more tightly about the piece of metal. 'Just say what you have to say and then go, please.'

'Lallie,' his sherry brown eyes, set under heavy

arched eyebrows slid over her, missing nothing, 'I'm not discussing private business with you on an open landing. Open the door like a good girl and we'll go inside where you can get out of those wet things, make us a cup of tea and we'll have the talk I came here to have with you.'

'I've nothing to say to you.' She raised her small chin and attempted to step past him, but he reached out to grasp her hand, prising her clutching fingers apart and extracting the small key.

'That's better—in with you now,' and he slid the key into the lock, pushed the door open, put a hand on her shoulder and impelled her inside. The door closed behind them and she shrugged off his hand and walked before him, through the small lobby and into the living room which, with the divan stripped of its daytime cushions and gay crocheted wool rug, served as a bedroom.

'Comfortable if constricted,' Owen acknowledged, looking around him before crossing to the gas fire, lighting it and turning it on full.

'Quite comfortable,' she agreed dryly, 'and the bathroom's in there,' she nodded at one of the two facing doors, 'if you want to wash your hands.'

When he had vanished through the door, she took off her mac and boots, stuffed her feet into a pair of high-heeled pumps and then went back into the lobby where she hung up the mac and tossed the boots on the floor. When he returned from the bathroom, she was in the kitchenette, unpacking her canvas carrier and outwardly composed.

Owen put his head round the door and gave the cupboards, the counter, the sink and draining board and the small gas cooker a swift, assessing scrutiny. 'You actually cook in this cupboard?'

Lallie went to crouch by the little fridge, her back to him as she packed away her perishables, and her teeth closed on the soft flesh of her lower lip. 'We're not all as well blessed as you, Owen!' Try as she would, she couldn't stop a shrillness from colouring her voice. 'Tea, did you say?' And she rose from her crouch and reached for the kettle to fill it.

'Mmm,' he still lounged against the door jamb, watching her movements, 'and a meal, if you can run to it. We haven't a lot of time and I'd like for us to leave as soon as possible. It'll take us the best part of seven hours to get home and I've got a surgery at half past ten tomorrow morning.'

Lallie looked at him consideringly before she lit the gas jet under the kettle. He hadn't changed much in nearly six years, maybe he looked a bit older and there were a few flecks of grey in his reddish hair, but that was all. Now that he stood in a good light, he no longer looked devilish, just hard and uncompromising. It was a severe face, but the severity was softened by the sensuous curve of his rather full bottom lip, although his chin looked as though it had been carved out of something stony and enduring.

She continued her inspection down over his tweed jacket, fawn cord trousers and bulky, well polished brogues; it gave her time to crowd down her emotions and present him with a calm front. It would never do to let him see she was afraid.

'A meal?' She shrugged. 'I've got a cooked chicken, frozen chips and a tin of peas, if that's any good to you and if it will save you wasting any more time—

but what do you mean? *We* haven't time—It'll take *us* seven hours? I'm not going anywhere with you, in fact,' her eyes started to glow golden with temper, 'I wouldn't go to the end of the road with you!' Her voice had become saccharine sweet, but bitterness and a grim determination showed through.

'You're needed.' He ignored the sweetness, the bitterness and the grim determination as though they hadn't even registered with him. 'That's why I'm here—to fetch you, so hurry up, Lallie. Like I said . . .'

'. . . and like I said,' she interrupted fiercely, 'I'm not going with you. Why should I? The only place I'm going is to work tomorrow morning as usual!'

'No, you're not,' he shook his head at her reprovingly. 'I phoned your office. You'd gone, but they put me through to your boss. As a special favour, he's giving you some unpaid leave, as much as you want. You're coming home!'

'Owen,' she mocked his reproving tone, 'you're getting old! Your wits have gone wandering. *This* is my home, it has been for nearly six years, ever since I left that *nice* couple you boarded me with. I've got this and a decent job, and I'm not giving any of it up to go off into the wide blue yonder with you, no matter who needs me. I'll give you a meal, I'd do that for a stray dog, but when you've eaten it, you can get lost as far as I'm concerned!'

'Still smarting?' He raised a hand to push back a lock of the reddish hair which had fallen over his forehead.

'As you say,' she sounded weary. 'I'm still smarting, and who wouldn't be? The last time I saw you, the atmosphere wasn't what you'd call pleasant. If I remember rightly, you accused me of about everything your rotten mind could think of and you refused even to give me a hearing. You dragged me away from my friends and put me in the charge of a couple who were no better than gaolers to me!'

Her hand, holding the lighted match to the gas jets in the oven, shook so much they refused to light and she squeaked as the match burned down to her fingers. The little pain caused her control to slip away so that tears started into her eyes, but she still had enough sense not to let them fall—Owen pounced on any sign of weakness like a cat on a mouse. So she scrambled to her feet and turned her back on him, becoming very busy putting the chicken in a fireproof dish and finding the chip pan and a saucepan for the peas.

'Like I said, I'll give you a meal, but that's all you're getting from me. There's a tin of rice pudding for afters, if you want it.' She heard herself speaking normally and was pleased.

'Does everything you eat come out of a packet or a tin?' She might as well not have spoken for all the attention he paid to what she had said. 'No wonder you look half starved!'

Lallie now had her emotions under iron control so that she could turn to him with the ghost of a sweet smile plastered on her face. 'Do you want the rice pudding?'

'Any jam to put on it?'

She gave a snort of disgust and opened the cutlery drawer. 'Here, lay the table,' and she thrust a load of cutlery into his hands, crowning the pile with a tablecloth. 'I'll be as quick as I can,' she assured him, 'not only because I don't wish to delay you but also because I can't stand the sight of you,' and she turned away to struggle with the polythene wrapping of the packet of frozen chips.

'The only way you'll delay me,' the look he gave her was dark and menacing, 'is to be your usual, obstinate, pigheaded little self. I didn't want to say anything, not yet—there's no point in your worrying for any longer than is strictly necessary, but since you're being so damned unco-operative, it's Dwynwen!'

'Dwynny?' She choked back on surprise. Owen's ageing housekeeper had always seemed like the Rock of Gibraltar, ageless and enduring for ever. 'What's the matter with Dwynny?'

'Old age, high blood pressure, overweight and just recently, a bit of quite needless worry—oh, nothing to do with you, so don't blame yourself. She's had a heart attack.'

Lallie dropped the pan of oil so quickly that it splashed over, spotting her fingers and the floor by the gas cooker, and she looked up at him with wide, frightened eyes. 'Is it serious?'

'At her age, it's bound to be,' and he walked off with his burden to lay the table, leaving her standing by the cooker with a worried frown on her face. She tipped the can of peas into a saucepan, lit the gas ring under them and hurried into the living room.

'You don't understand, do you?' she was bitter. 'After the way you treated me, practically shutting the door in my face, I started to make my own life here. I found this flat and I found a good job—I'm independent . . .'

'Little Miss Independence!' It was almost a sneer. 'How do you like working for old Tommy Griffiths?'

'You know him?' Humiliation swept over her at his nod. He wasn't leaving her anything of her much vaunted independence, not even the consolation of having found a good job on her own merits.

'My godfather,' Owen's smile wasn't nice, it was mean and triumphant. 'He's gone up in the world since he ran the Aber branch of the insurance company.' He was amused at her chagrin, and then he relented. 'Don't look so woebegone, you little idiot! He wrote saying he'd had an application from you, he recognised your name—he asked if I would give you a character reference—you only had one and he needed another. I simply wrote back saying that as far as I was concerned, you were of good character, dependable and trustworthy, and you were also a good typist.'

Chagrin was replaced by temper, her eyes flashed and her soft mouth hardened into a straight, thin line. 'You won't leave me anything, will you? Not even the least, littlest thing! I said you were a bastard . . .'

'Don't swear, Lallie,' he snapped. 'It doesn't become you. Tommy took you on as a typist and he's not one to play favourites. What you've achieved since is entirely on your own merits—nothing to do with me. And I didn't tell him about anything else, either. Your little secret is quite safe, he doesn't know a thing about it and he won't unless . . .'

'Unless I don't do as I'm told, is that it?'

'That's precisely it,' he nodded agreeably. 'Now, let's get this meal over, then you can throw a few things into a case and we'll go.'

Lallie flounced back into the kitchenette, skidded on a dribble of oil and squealed in mingled pain and temper as a hot pain shot through her ankle as her foot twisted beneath her and she sat down on the vinyl-tiled floor with a bump. 'Now look what you've made me do!' she yelled wrathfully.

'I've made you do nothing.' He came calmly to stoop beside her. 'Where does it hurt?'

'My foot, you idiot!' and as he stooped over her, feeling around her ankle with cool fingers and moving her foot from side to side, she squealed again. 'Don't do that, it hurts!'

'Stop yelling,' he commanded. 'It's only a bit of a wrench, hardly enough to be called a sprain.' He put his hand under her instep and pushed upwards gently, and she repressed her yell into a faint squeak.

'I know it's not a sprain,' she said through set teeth, losing most of her control. 'It's broken! How would you know what it is? You're not a doctor, you're only a vet. I want it X-rayed.'

'You want a cup of tea and an aspirin,' he corrected, and she envied him his calm so much, she felt like weeping as he picked her up and carried her into the living room to sit her on a chair. 'Sit there while I make the tea and rescue the dinner, then I'll bathe it for you, strap it up and and we'll eat. Stop trying to delay things, Lallie, it's not half as bad as you make out. You'll come home with me, stay with Dwynwen till she's better, run the house for her and put her mind at rest about her little problem. Then you'll be free to come back here. I'm not taking you into unknown territory, you've lived there before.'

Which was quite true; she'd gone to live at Bryn Celyn, a remote place near the Dyffy valley when she was four years old—when her mother had married Owen's father. She'd been too young to remember anything much about the flat in Pimlico where she had been born, all her memories were of Bryn Celyn—the farmhouse and its huddle of barns and outhouses in the secret little valley, the sheep on the hills, the stream bordered with birches and rowans and the holly trees from which the house took its name. It had been a wonderful place to grow up in and Owen, ten years older than herself, had been the kindest big brother in the world. There had been Jonty as well, only eight at the time, and Dorcas, their sister who was only a year older than herself.

But it wasn't her home, not her real home, and Dorcas wasn't her real sister, that was made plain to her on the first day she started school—when they had all sat in the the classroom while their names were read out. 'Dorcas Tudor', and Dorcas had stood up in the desk she was sharing with Lallie, and then she'd hauled Lallie to her feet. The mistress had smiled at her and said, 'Oh, the new little English girl, Alison Moncke', which had made her feel different as though she didn't really belong. After that, she hadn't liked the school very much and she hadn't co-operated when they tried to teach her Welsh. If she was different, she would *be* different!

When she was fourteen, her mother and Daddy Tudor had been killed in a road accident and there had been only Dwynwen to comfort her. Dorcas and

Jonty had each other and Owen was away at veterinary college, so she had clung to Dwynwen and they had helped each other . . . Lallie stopped reminiscing at this point to watch Owen bring in the tea.

'Nothing burned,' he assured her. 'It's all ready, but we'll see to that ankle first. Aspirin and a bandage?'

'First aid box in the bathroom,' she said curtly. 'It should all be in there, I've never opened it since I bought it,' and she leaned back in the chair and closed her eyes. Her ankle was hurting like mad, her head was aching and she felt sick. She wanted Owen to go, he brought back all the memories she'd buried—all the things she didn't want to remember—the things which hurt so much more than her ankle.

But he wouldn't go, she knew that, not until he'd got what he came for. Owen had always been the same, he had an idea and plugged away at it until it had stopped being an idea and become a fact—an accomplished thing. He called her pig-headed, but compared with him, she was nothing!

He came back to her with the plastic bucket she used to mop the kitchenette floor, setting it down at her feet and putting the bandage beside it. 'Stocking or tights?' he enquired.

'Tights,' she muttered, leaning over to dip a finger in the bucket of water. It was icy cold and she shivered.

'Get 'em off, I can't bandage on top of these,' and she hopped on one foot while she wriggled them down over her hips. Owen seemed to take a fiendish delight in plunging her foot into the ice-cold water and holding it here until it was nearly numb.

'No aspirin,' he was cheerful about it. 'But it's better if you can manage without. Wipe it dry,' and he handed her the towel which he'd brought draped over his shoulder while he opened the packet of bandage. 'Comfortable now?' He stood back to admire his handiwork and then scooped her up to carry her to the table. Lallie had to admit that the strapping looked very neat and professional, but it was much too tight. Beneath it, her ankle throbbed and she felt sick with the pain as she was seated at the table, knowing she wouldn't be able to eat.

'What use shall I be?' she demanded sulkily. 'I can't walk.'

He grinned at her cheerfully. 'Stop feeling sorry for yourself, *cariad*. It's only a minor sprain, in a couple of days you'll not notice it. What's the matter, can't you eat?' as she stared miserably at her plate.

'No, I don't want anything,' her eyes slid to the divan. 'Could I lie down until you're finished? I've just remembered, there's some paracetamol in my bag, I could have a couple of those with another cup of tea and perhaps I'd sleep for a bit and maybe feel better.'

'Good idea.' Owen rooted in her bag himself for the tablets and brought them to her with a fresh cup. 'Drink up and I'll carry you to the couch.'

When she woke, the curtains were drawn and the room was in darkness, lit only by the glow of the gas fire. She stirred drowsily and became aware that her quarters were more cramped than usual. There was another big body lying beside her on the divan and a heavy arm about her waist. She struggled up, wincing as her foot moved and she pushed at Owen's wide chest. 'What in hell do you think you're doing?' It came out as a savagely indignant whisper, she didn't shout because some of the walls of the flat were no more than paper-thin partitions.

Owen opened his eyes. There was no brief period when he had to orientate himself, remember where he was—his eyes opened, he was awake and glaring at her.

'I'm catching up on some sleep I shall miss,' he growled. 'I started out just after seven this morning, I've driven down here and in an hour or so I have to drive back. That'll be over five hundred miles in one day. Do you grudge me a corner of your couch? And don't look so offended, I was too tired to make a pass at you, and if I had, what are you complaining about? This won't be the first time you've been to bed with a man.'

Lallie deliberately shut the words from her mind—ignoring them as though they'd never been said. Instead she concentrated on her ankle as it joggled about. 'How's Dwynwen?' she asked in a chill little voice. 'She is going to get better, isn't she?'

'You're actually interested?' He sat on the side of the divan, rubbing his face gently with his hand as though he would rub the tiredness away. 'I've been thinking you'd grown too callous to care. It was touch and go for a while—the first couple of days were dicey, but she's over the worst. Now, shift yourself, little one, we've wasted enough time. If I carry you over to that cupboard, do you think you could throw a few things in a case?' As he was speaking, he rose to his feet and lifted her, jogging her foot even more so that she squealed.

'It *is* broken,' she gasped. 'Never mind about taking me back with you, take me to a hospital!'

'If you don't stop making so much fuss about a trifling sprain, I'll take you to a knacker's yard,' he threatened. Then, as he saw the extent of the swelling, 'I wish we'd had a wider bandage, that one's too small, too narrow to do the job properly.'

'You mean you don't carry these necessities with you?' She said sarcastically, muttering the words into his shoulder as he carried her across the room. 'How remiss of you, Owen! You never know when you might need these little things, you might meet a horse with a splint or something, you should be prepared.'

'Shut up!' he warned her, 'or I'll slap your backside, you aggravating little madam.' He dumped her in a chair and reached down a small suitcase. 'Here, put some clothes in that while I make us another cup of tea.'

Soothed by the tea and another paracetamol, Lallie found herself installed in Owen's beloved old Bentley, its age apparent only in its flowing lines. She watched him turn on his famous smile for her landlady, saw them talking under the street lamp—saw the woman's look of pleasure and gratification, and she ground her small white teeth. Another victim of the 'Owen Tudor' charm! One lopsided smile and seventy-five per cent of the female population swooned at his feet. She had had watched it happen ever since she could remember, even her own mother had fallen for it, to be extra kind and nice to him.

At about the age of fifteen, Lallie had decided to be one of the unswooning twenty-five per cent, and she had kept that promise which she had made to herself. She had never swooned, smile or no. Instead she had doled out large dollops of bitter sarcasm—treated him to caustic and biting comments and had driven him up the wall with an insolent disobedience— which in her opinion was just where he belonged— on top of a wall like any other randy tomcat!

She sank back into the soft leather upholstery as the car started away from the kerb, and then, because she was curious, 'Why couldn't Dorcas have come?'

'Baby on the way,' he said tersely, 'and a bit of difficulty with it. She's not built right for childbearing, too narrow in the pelvis. The doctors and specialists in Cardiff think she'll need a Caesarian, they're keeping a pretty watchful eye on her.'

'But why me? Why the black sheep? It's not as though you're short of real relations, you've got hundreds, the whole area's snithing with them!'

'Because Dwynwen asked for you and you owe her, you ungrateful brat. That's why—and now stop talking while I find my way out of London and on to the M1.'

Lallie closed her eyes and pretended to sleep while her mind went back to when she was fifteen. That had been when things started going downhill as regarded family relationships. Her mother and her stepfather were dead, Jonty just wasn't old enough at nineteen to have the responsibility of the farm, so Owen had given up the veterinary post he'd just obtained in South Wales and had come home to run

Bryn Celyn. He'd not confined his energies to the farm with the milking herd, the beef cattle and the sheep. He'd taken on a bit of veterinary work as well and he'd decided that his immediate family needed a bit of discipline. He'd taken one look at Lallie, heard just one of her tempestuous outbursts and had put his foot down, hard!

She was the first to admit that she'd been a bit spoiled, she was clever and quicker than either Jonty or Dorcas and she was always up to her neck in trouble, but that had been no reason, to her way of thinking, for Owen to take an immediate dislike to her, but he did and he showed it. She couldn't understand it, she had never disliked him, in fact she had been rather proud of him, but if he wanted it that way, that was the way he should have it, and the old house had become a battlefield where two generals had conducted a series of tactical exercises without troops, trying to get the better of each other. There hadn't been any blood or corpses on the battle-ground, Jonty, Dorcas and Dwynwen had never taken sides—it had been single combat.

When she had brought home poor school reports in the past, Daddy Tudor had never been cross, he didn't think very much of schooling. He admitted frankly that he'd never had very much himself and had done quite well without it, and he'd never told her mother either! Owen wasn't so sanguine. Lallie had a brain, therefore she should use it, not waste it, so there were no more carefree evenings when she ran and played with Jonty and the dogs or watched panel games on T.V. Instead, she had been forced to sit at the kitchen table, under Owen's eye, scribbling away like mad and missing all the fun. When she had presented him with only five 'O' levels, he had snorted down his masterful nose, saying it wasn't good enough.

'Why?' she had demanded, facing him across the desk in his office, the room he used for his clerical work. 'It's more than Jonty or Dorcas passed. Jonty only had three and Dorcas didn't even try, so why make a fuss about my five?'

'Because you're intelligent,' he had rasped at her. 'Jonty worked hard for those three, but you've simply idled through, you could have had eight if you'd put your mind to it. You've got two more years in school and I want two "A" level passes from you, good ones, and then we'll see about university.'

'I don't want . . .' but he had stopped her.

'I don't care what you want, you'll work!'

And she had beaten him on that as well. Only one 'A' level, and when the results had come out, she had glared at him triumphantly and gone off to a secretarial college, full of victory and self-satisfaction. At nineteen, she had gone to London to a job with a small firm run by a lady from Whitechapel. She had typed manuscripts, plays, theses, anything in fact which needed typing. The other four girls in the office had been nice to work with, the work was varied, it wasn't monotonous and she had been happy for a year.

Then, she had been foolish, that was the word for it. She hadn't done anything wrong, she had simply been young and too naïve for words—she skipped over this part quickly, it was painful, and so had been the follow-up.

Owen had come up to Town to forcibly remove her from the flat which she was sharing with two other girls, and he'd put her in lodgings with what he'd called 'people he could trust'. Gorgons, both of them! He'd also found her another job. She had stayed in both lodgings and job for a year, miserable with the monotony and the supervision, and she'd saved like mad until she had enough money to leave—to find her little flat and the work in the insurance office in Potters Bar.

Owen hadn't been either kind or understanding when her bit of trouble had happened. He'd been hard, angry and contemptuous, he hadn't even bothered to listen to her stumbling explanation—her little 'affair', as he called it, had been given a lot of publicity and he had believed the newspapers. She was no longer welcome at Bryn Celyn, although he graciously gave permission for her to write to Dwynwen. It had hurt her terribly and she had vowed then never to see or have anything to do with him again. She would manage on her own, and she *had* managed—she'd managed very well, and what was the end result of all her hard work and effort? Nothing! Here she was, on the way back to a place she'd vowed she'd never visit again, and in the company of the one man she'd promised herself she'd never speak to!

CHAPTER TWO

'ANKLE hurting?' Owen had pulled into a motorway services area and Lallie nodded, her face white in the neon lights of the parking ground.

'Mmm, a bit.' She put out a hand imploringly. 'Don't get me anything to eat, please, I feel sick.'

'You aren't getting anything to eat,' came his brutal reply. 'You can have a glass of milk, I don't want you throwing up in my car.'

Lallie wondered, and not for the first time, how he was able to alternate so quickly between kindness and downright bad manners, and came to the conclusion that he probably had a filthy liver or an enlarged spleen, although perhaps he'd had to break a date to come and fetch her. At this last thought, she smiled nastily.

'Not even a sugar lump or a pat on the head?' she enquired in dulcet tones. 'My, my, Owen, you're slipping!'

She watched him stalk off towards the services and her mouth curved into a smile. Outright defiance made him worse, sulkiness seemed to amuse him so that he treated her as though she was five years old again, but catty little remarks seemed to get under his skin. So when she had finished the plastic tot of milk which he brought her, she rested her head on the back of the seat, closed her eyes and thought up some more needling remarks which could be used when the occasion demanded.

In the middle of one such remark, she fell asleep and woke up at the next stop, a transport café—one of the all-night ones on the Welshpool road, well past Shrewsbury. And there was Owen standing over her with a huge mug of hot tomato soup.

'Try this,' he advised. 'It's hot—and then you can go back to sleep while it's still dark. It'll be breaking dawn in a couple of hours.'

'Mmm, nice.' She finished the soup and felt like asking for more, it put a nice glow in her stomach and the heat of the thick mug warmed her fingers. Somehow, he managed to pick up her thought.

'No more. The first one's always good, but any more and you'd be finding fault, saying it was out of a packet or a tin.'

Lallie didn't want to sleep, she thought it better to stay awake, to talk just in case Owen felt sleepy himself, so she chatted in a sugary fashion with just a soupçon of vinegar at the back of it.

'Who have you got coming in to look after us two invalids?' she asked sweetly. 'You're going to regret fetching me, aren't you?'

'There'll be nobody coming to look after you, Lallie,' he grinned at her. 'That little sprain, it won't bother you much providing you don't do daft things like tottering around in those stupid high heels you wear and Nerys Roberts comes up from the village every day, eight till five, so all you'll have to do is to oversee her and do a bit of cooking. As for regretting bringing you,' he slid her a glance which was unfathomable, 'Dwynwen wants you, that's all that matters to me.'

'I shall do the supervision from my invalid chair,' she snapped, then softened. 'Tell me what's been going on at Bryn Celyn since I left. Dwynwen writes once a month, as you probably know, I suspect you censor her letters—but they, the letters, aren't all that informative. How's Jonty?'

'Living at the old Jones' sheep farm. I bought it last year when the old man died. There's a lot of room there and Jonty was wanting to go in for pigs as well as the sheep, but I'm sorry to say he's blotted his copybook as far as Dwynwen's concerned.'

'No wonder Dwynny hasn't mentioned him!' She pulled a face. 'What's he done?'

Owen took his attention from the road for a moment to slant a speculative glance at her. In the light of the dashboard it made him look demonic, then he turned his attention back to the road.

'Three months ago he took on one of those agricultural students, a girl who wanted to learn a little more about sheep, and she's moved in with him. Dwynwen thinks they're living in sin!'

'And are they?'

He shrugged carelessly. 'Who knows? Maybe, maybe not, it's their own business.'

This was Lallie's opportunity and she grabbed it with both hands. 'It runs in the family, doesn't it? Jonty has a shepherdess full time and you go in for "conferences"—what's the difference? Dwynwen never got hot under the collar about you, so why put Jonty on the black list?'

'I was discreet.' He sounded smug.

'And that makes it better?' The smugness upset her and she snorted down her small, straight nose.

'You're all two-faced, that's what's the matter with you. Anything's acceptable as long as it's done in private. Was that what upset you so much about my little bit of trouble—the publicity? Would you have turned a blind eye if it hadn't been splashed all over the newspapers? "Leading actress in new play threatens to walk out on her husband, producer, because of shabby little affair with pert young typist". I wouldn't have minded so much if I'd done anything wrong, but you wouldn't believe me. Now I see why—I'd broken the cardinal rule, "Never be found out"!'

'Nobody else believed you either,' Owen pointed out calmly.

Lallie closed her lips firmly on the hot words bubbling up in her throat. Let Owen think what he liked, it didn't hurt much any more, and she didn't have to justify herself to him. Compared with him, she was a stainless lily. She'd been conned, in the nicest possible way and by an expert who knew how to set the stage and exactly what words to use. They'd needed some extra publicity for the play, it hadn't been getting enough coverage in the press and she had walked into a situation deliberately set up, contrived to get them that maximum coverage needed before the play opened. A front page spread in every London daily with follow-ups, interviews and pictures in which Marla Lake, the star, was beautifully distressed and dreadfully hurt by her husband's infidelity. The kettle had been kept on the boil for over a week before Marla forgave all and her producer husband had her back as the star of his show and the wife of his bosom.

Marla and her husband had both been very discreet, of course—never was the name of the 'pert little typist' mentioned, but the gentlemen of the press had fastened on the scent and Lallie's anonymity hadn't lasted very long. When the bomb burst, she had gone to the boss, the Whitechapel lady, and tendered her resignation, but her boss had raised her eyebrows, passed a heavily beringed hand over her titian dyed hair and told her to go home and have a re-think, while admitting that it was partly her fault in allowing Lallie to do outside work on the script alterations during rehearsals.

'But Marla's husband chose you, my dear, and after all, you'd already done a lot of the work on the script, work which he said was very good. Think no more about it, I knew what they were up to as soon as I saw the papers that first day. Just a cheap and effective way of getting publicity—but by then it was too late.'

So Lallie had continued working despite a great deal of harassment from the press until Owen had come up to London and hauled her away by the scruff of her neck.

But Owen had believed, that was what had hurt worst, and she had the idea she would never forgive him for that, nor for the things he had said to her!

It was just before dawn when Owen pulled into the farmyard at Bryn Celyn and Lallie, who had gone to sleep after all, blinked drowsily and roused herself enough to open her door and scramble out on to the cobbles of the yard, wincing as she tried to put some weight on her foot. Owen slammed his own door and came round the car to look at her. 'Forget it,' he ordered peremptorily as she hopped away from him. 'I'll carry you.'

Lallie would have loved to say 'Over my dead body', but she had to be practical. The cobbles of the yard stretched in front of her like an ocean and after them came the crazy paving up through the sloping garden to the house. She was never going to manage it, not without wrenching her ankle again.

'The wheelbarrow,' she said brightly, nodding to where one stood against the wall of the barn. 'Put me and my case in that and wheel me up to the door.'

'We've been carting muck in it—but if you insist . . .' He was jeering at her, and she changed her mind swiftly. For some reason, she was feeling extraordinarily happy, and the happiness bred a confidence in her. Whatever happened, she felt she could cope with it, come up smiling.

'Carry me, then, Owen dear.' There was a syrupy sweetness in her voice—she almost coohed. 'Pretend I'm your newly wedded wife—your bride, and you're taking me home . . .' Her words were cut off abruptly as he grasped her and swung her over his shoulder in a fireman's lift, but she wasn't silenced. 'A bride, I said, not a sack of spuds!' she gasped and then, 'Damn, my hair's fallen down and I've lost all my hairpins. Owen!' as he pushed open the gate on to the crazy paving. 'Carry me properly, please!'

'Then stop wagging that filthy little tongue,' he snapped brusquely as he lowered her to the ground and lifted her up into his arms. 'You're a bitter little thing, Lallie. What you need is a damn good hiding, and you're going the right way to get it!'

'Caveman!' she jeered softly, and her arms tightened round his neck desperately as she felt his loosen their grip on her. 'No, Owen, please. I didn't mean it, honestly!'

'There's a nice apology,' he grinned down at her in the growing light. 'About the first I've ever wrenched out of you. Shut up!' He released one arm to open the door and brought the free hand up to cover her mouth, swearing when she sank her teeth into his thumb.

'A bitter, *biting* little thing,' she hissed as he set her down in the hallway, 'and don't bother helping me any more, I'll crawl first!'

'And I'll have an extra tetanus shot first thing,' he snapped back at her. 'There's enough poison in your spit to kill the entire population!'

Lallie ignored him and hopped off down the passage to the kitchen door, pushing it open and making her way to the big rocking chair which stood by the solid fuel cooker. She slumped into it gratefully and moaned at the sight of her foot. Her ankle, as an ankle, had ceased to exist.

'Look at that!' she demanded. 'That's your slight sprain! The one I'm going to be able to walk on tomorrow.'

'Stop it, nuisance.' Owen sounded weary as he filled the kettle and switched it on, and she looked at him over her shoulder. The chestnut in his hair was much more prominent under the overhead light, but there was a grey look of tiredness on his face, the lines from his nose to his mouth seemed to be cut more deeply and his brows were drawn together over his eyes. 'I'm tired, girl. I haven't the energy or the inclination to spar with you now. You slept most of the way while I was driving, remember?'

'Mmm,' she was prepared to be generous. 'I'll give you a chance to have a rest before battle commences.'

'Thanks.' He warmed the teapot and added tea before collecting cups from the dresser shelf.

'And I'll have a cup of tea and snooze here by the fire while you go to bed for a couple of hours,' she offered. 'Does Dwynny have an early cuppa?'

'No, don't disturb her.' His head was bent over the teapot and his voice was hushed to almost a whisper. 'And don't make too much noise, keep your voice down, she hears every sound. We won't bother her until later in the morning, after the nurse has been. I want to have a little talk with you first, there are some things you have to know.'

'Aha!' Her voice started on its normal tone and then dropped to a whisper under his glare. 'So it's not so straightforward after all! What have you been up to, Owen—is it you who's upset Dwynny?'

'I told you, it's a combination of things—her age, her physical condition, worry over Jonty,' he brought her a cup. 'Drink that and leave the questions till later. You can have a few hours in bed yourself, but I'll see to that ankle first.'

'You're wriggling,' Lallie accused in a gleeful whisper. 'There's more than that and I bet you're at the bottom of it. Hoo!' she broke into soft, mocking laughter and sipped her tea with an enjoyment she hadn't felt for ages. 'Owen the Mighty descending to stratagems—but you don't have to worry, do you?' She raised her long grey-gold eyes to his face, they were not laughing now, they held a faint glow of contempt. 'You've always got little Lallie. You can bully little Lallie into helping you out of the mess you've dropped yourself in! Well, let me tell you, my lad, little Lallie's grown up and she's not half as stupid as she used to be and she's way past bullying.' Her voice had risen slightly and he stopped it with a hard hand over her mouth.

'Drink your tea,' he hissed, 'and I'll carry you upstairs. Nobody's bullying anybody. Dwynwen needs you—and that's an appeal to your better nature, if you have one. She was very good to you when our parents died and despite everything, she still thinks the world of you, she trusts you. Now, come on, *cariad*, let's have you upstairs and I'll see to that ankle.'

'I'll never be able to walk on it.' Lallie was sitting on the edge of her bed and Owen was just finishing the fresh strapping. She looked down at his head where he was intent on getting the bandage good and tight, and on impulse she put out a hand to his hair. He felt her soft touch and raised his head.

'Is that a thank-you?'

'Certainly not!' All her belligerence returned in a wave of self-distrust. 'You're getting to be quite an old man, Owen, I was just looking at your grey hairs.'

'You put them there, if it's any consolation to you,' he retorted. 'I've brought up your case, so get yourself into a nightie and give that tongue of yours a rest for a couple of hours. And you *will* be able to walk on that foot, you haven't pulled a tendon or anything serious, so stop playing the invalid. Just don't wear unsuitable shoes or try flopping round in slippers. You need a bit of support for a couple of days, that's all.'

'I'd get more help from a proper doctor,' she grumbled. 'He'd have given me some pills and sympathy.'

'Poor little thing!' Owen bent his head over her and his mouth found hers in a gentle kiss. 'Mmm,' when he raised his head, 'I should have tried that before, it keeps you quiet.' And the door closed behind him, leaving her looking at the panels while one finger touched her lips.

Oh yes, Owen had it all, he could charm the birds from the trees when he put his mind to it. No wonder he was such a howling success at 'conferences'! But he wasn't going to be allowed to charm her. Her eyes slitted with determination and her mouth firmed as she hobbled to her case and extracted a clean nightie. Owen wanted her co-operation in something and he wasn't going to get it, not unless he went down on his knees and begged for it. She owed herself that—it would be balm to her wounded spirit!

'Wake up, sleepyhead!' That was Owen being full of life and energy, and she glared at him and then at her watch she'd forgotten to wind.

'What time is it?' she grumbled. She'd been having a lovely dream, although she couldn't remember what it was about, and if nobody had disturbed her, she could have slept for the rest of the day.

'Half past one. I've just come back from the surgery in Trellwyd.' He nodded to the old-fashioned washstand. 'I've brought you in some hot water from the bathroom, so wash and dress yourself and don't take too long about it. I'll be back in ten minutes to take you downstairs.'

Carrying her easily, he went past the door to his office and headed for the kitchen, but she tapped him on the shoulder.

'I thought you said we were going to have a talk?'

'After lunch, I think.' He kept on walking. 'Nerys is willing, but she's a long way from being a good cook. I'm trying to catch her before she chars the steak and burns the chips.'

'So,' she mused. 'I'm to be the cook, am I? What does Dwynny have, surely not steak and chips?'

'Invalid food mostly.' He pushed open the kitchen door, walked across and dumped her in a chair by the table. 'It's varied with steamed fish or beef tea, that sort of thing,' and he stopped speaking as Nerys came in with a dish of steaks and chips There wasn't much conversation after that, since Nerys joined them at the table and Lallie knew all about the girl's mother who kept the post office in the village and who was the biggest gossip this side of the Severn.

Nerys herself didn't gossip, she was a sponge which absorbed information, she soaked it up, stored it and retailed every bit to her mother, but as Dwynny said, she was a good worker.

The meal over, Lallie brushed a few crumbs from her grey pleated skirt, smoothed back a few tendrils of black hair which were tickling the tops of her ears and stood up uncertainly. She waved away Owen's proffered help with an ungracious hand.

'I can walk—it may take a little longer, but that's your fault. You made me slip, so you'll just have to put up with it. Where are we going for this famous talk, your office?'

'It's out of earshot,' he murmured, making allowances for Nerys' ears which would be pricked for the slightest sound. 'And we don't want it getting round the district that, as well as her other shortcomings, little Lallie has a tongue like a fishwife, do we?'

'Brilliant tactics,' she muttered as she went slowly along the passage. As he had predicted, she could walk without too much pain, but since he'd said it, she wasn't going to let him know he was right, so she gasped a bit and wore a pained expression as she hobbled along, and once in the office, she slid into the chair opposite his desk with a loud moan of relief, but her little act didn't get the applause it deserved, neither did it stir Owen to any tender feelings.

'Putting on the agony?' And his smile was dangerous. 'Stop appealing for sympathy, girl. I've known a horse run with a worse sprain than you have.'

Lallie bridled and flushed a bit. 'Talk!' she snapped. 'There's something very fishy here, I can smell it a mile off. What is this "needless" worry, this "little" problem? Aha!' she crowed as she saw his mouth tighten. 'It's something to do with you! Come on, Owen, confess. You can, you know, being so depraved myself, I shall understand.'

'In a way,' he was grudging. 'I suppose you could say I'm to blame.'

'Oh, I shall say it,' Lallie's eyes sparkled with a gloating satisfaction. 'But *do* continue . . .'

'. . . then be quiet while I think of the best way to put it . . .'

'. . . so it won't make you look too bad?'

'Lallie!' It was a warning growl and she knew from experience that she'd pushed him far enough—as far as it was safe. It would be more politic, at this point, to be quiet in case she went too far and he errupted into a blunt, flaying savagery. She lowered her eyes demurely and folded her hands in her lap, but her busy tongue got the better of her.

'Tell all,' she said with sarcasm. 'Let little Lallie in on the ground floor. Who knows, if you appeal to my sympathy, I may be tempted to help.'

'It started last October.' Owen fiddled with a pencil. 'I was in Aber and I met a girl I was in school with. She married an Army bloke and he died a while back, so she came home, hoping to get a job around here. She has a small pension, but not enough to live on, and it was the wrong time of the year for finding work in Aber. She's had some experience in catering and so forth, but as you know, a lot of the hotels in the area close for the winter—she just wanted something to keep her going until spring.'

'. . . And out of the goodness of your heart and the corruption of your morals, you offered her a job here. What was she to be, your assistant housekeeper with fringe benefits for a kind employer?'

'London hasn't improved you,' he said with emphasis. 'You want your mouth washed out with soap, so shut up or I'll do it.' And it wasn't an empty threat, she knew. He was quite capable of carrying it out, he'd done it before when she was little. 'As I said, I offered her a job. I'm the county vet and I don't have time for the paper work of the farm. I thought she could cope with that and maybe give

Dwynwen a hand. It was time the old girl took things a bit more easily.'

'Tell me no more,' Lallie waved a hand. 'You don't have to say another word. But what happened, did Dwynny catch you in bed with her or did the lady get more permanent ideas and start easing Dwynny out—perhaps suggesting that she should retire completely?'

'You're on the right track,' he admitted, and she was surprised to see that his smile was slightly rueful. 'The lady had very permanent ideas, but not because she occupies my bed, she doesn't. The one time when I've been quite altruistic with not an evil thought in my mind!'

'It's your reputation, Owen, it goes before you,' she murmured. 'Where is the lady now, have you got rid of her?'

Owen shook his head, 'She went on a fortnight's holiday just before Dwynwen collapsed, she's due back on Monday . . .'

'. . . All bright and sparkling and waiting with bated breath for you to produce the ring?' Lallie couldn't help herself, she started giggling, the giggles turned to outright laughter and tears of mirth poured down her cheeks. 'S-serve you right! I've been waiting for something like this, but I thought you were too damn clever ever to be caught—that I'd never have the chance to crow over you.'

'You can stop crowing,' he scowled at her while his mouth lifted in a reluctant smile. 'This isn't the time for it, we have to work out a plan . . .'

'*We* have to work out a plan?' she interrupted fiercely. 'Oh no, Owen, *you* have to put things straight, I don't come into it at all. I wasn't here, I didn't know anything about it and I don't owe you anything, remember? I'll just stand by and watch you go down for the third time and I'll laugh while you're doing it. This *is* my time to crow. I've never forgotten the things you said to me, the names you called me or the way you wouldn't believe me. Now it's my turn to say I don't believe you. I'm not saying you ever had any permanent intentions because I know you too well. I'm sure you didn't, the "bachelor gay" life is too dear to you, but I suppose you couldn't keep your hands to yourself, so it serves you right. Get out of your own mess!'

There was an angry satisfaction in her voice and her eyes were slitted and gleaming with it.

'And Dwynwen,' he reminded her. 'You can take your spite out on me as much as you like, I can stand it—but there's Dwynwen. She has this mad idea that I'm going to put her in a home for geriatrics, that's what was the final straw. It made her heart attack almost inevitable.'

'Then you'll have to tell her you'll do no such thing . . .'

'I have,' he cut her off short and he was fierce about it. 'It didn't work, so . . .'

'She won't believe me either.' Lallie felt herself growing cold, she sensed danger. 'What had you in mind?'

'Simple.' Owen made a bit of a fuss about finding his pipe, filling it and using three matches to get it going while Lallie waited with growing impatience. 'You and I are engaged, but we shan't be getting married, not for six months or so.' He came round the desk and clapped his hand over her mouth. 'You have to be given time to see whether you could live here after being in the big city, you might miss the bright lights and your middle-aged beaux. At the end of that six months, you will of course decide you can't stand the place or me and it will be all over, but in that time, we'll have Dwynwen back on her feet and convinced she isn't going to be chucked on the scrap heap.' He removed his hand from her mouth and stood back. 'Now you can talk!'

'Six months!' Lallie exploded. 'You're out of your mind! What about my job and my flat? I couldn't live here and keep my flat going, I'd have to give it up and I couldn't ask my boss to keep my job open for that length of time.'

'He will,' Owen told her serenely. 'I asked him and he said so. Old Tommy's not a bad sort and he understands.'

'And my flat, what about that?' She thought she was weakening and made a more determined stand. 'I'd have to give it up, and what then? Have you any idea of how difficult it is to get a place in London? And in any case, what gives you the idea that Dwynny will believe me when she won't believe you?'

'Because she loves you, idiot. Oh yes, I know, she loves us all, but you've always been something special. You're her little white hen that never laid away.' He looked at her sardonically. 'She thought up every excuse in the book for you and it ended up with me in the dirt, I was to blame for what you did, it was *my* fault you'd fallen by the wayside. I'd always treated you harshly—I hadn't understood you—I'd driven you out into the wide world, alone and defenceless and into that sink of iniquity. Need I go on . . . ?'

Lallie sat very still and remembered. It seemed she did very little else but remember nowadays. She remembered Dwynwen's warm arms and the comfort of her sturdy body when her own mother had been killed, the housekeeper's unfailing kindness . . . Yes, she did owe, and she said as much in a quiet voice, looking not at Owen but somehow through him as her mind went ranging back to happier times.

'All right, Owen, I'll do it. Like you said, I owe,' and then she came back to the present and her soft mouth hardened. 'But don't forget, I owe you as well, and that's one debt I'm looking forward to paying with interest!'

He ignored the implied threat as though she had never made it and went fishing in the desk drawer to come out with a small, worn leather box. 'You'd better have this,' he tossed it across to her. 'It was my mother's and it should fit, she had very small hands. We want it to look genuine, don't we?'

'And it's the look of the thing that matters.' Her lips twisted into a bitter smile. 'Thanks for reminding me. Can we see Dwynny now?'

'Put the ring on first, she'll be expecting it.'

'Expecting it?' Her voice rose in wrath. 'Do you mean you've told her already, before you came to fetch me, is that it? Well, of all the unmitigated cheek . . . ! I've a good mind to refuse and let you stew in your own juice. You've actually made her think you could walk in on me, give me a call and I'd do whatever you want . . .'

'No,' he was wry. 'She'll only think that at last I've

come to my senses. She built up the fairy tale a long time ago. You and I were going to marry. Put on the ring, *cariad*, and we'll tell her that dreams do come true sometimes. Here, let me help you,' as she fumbled with the catch of the box and he slid the oval setting of rubies on a narrow gold band over her knuckle. 'Now, come along, I'll carry you, it'll look that much more romantic!'

He picked her up and she immediately slid both her arms round his neck, hanging on tightly. 'There's no need to strangle me,' he protested.

'Strangle you?' Lallie shook her head. 'As if I would! Strangling's too good for you, you deserve something a lot more slow and painful. No, I was trying to look like a bit of orange blossom. That's right, throw me on the floor in your temper! Tut, tut, you'll have to learn restraint, Mr Tudor, otherwise I shan't play your game. It needn't take longer than twenty-four hours for me to decide I'd die if I had to live here, then where would you be?'

'Your tongue's too busy again,' and he bent his head, silencing her with his mouth on hers, but this time there was nothing gentle or kind about it. The pressure was painful as he forced her lips apart and although she struggled, kicking out with her good foot, pummelling with her fists and trying to twist her head away from him, it had no effect. He was holding her as if she weighed no more than a baby and doing it with just one arm, while his free hand had fastened about her throat, his thumb seductively rubbing at the hollow behind her ear. When he raised his head, her eyes were wet and she could only whisper.

'Don't, Owen. Please don't do that to me.'

'Come off it, Lallie,' he looked down at her mockingly. 'You've been around, you know what it's all about, so why the virginal shrinking? I'm not impressed, if that was what you hoped for.'

'I won't play your game,' she threatened.

'Yes, you will, my girl. You'll play any damn game I choose, because if you don't, I'll stop playing games and start in for real. Then you can measure up my performance against your ageing Romeo.' He was only whispering, but there was menace in his every hiss and she closed her eyes against the feral gleam in his.

Sometimes, she told herself, it was better to stop fighting—safer. And this was one of those times, but even so, she wasn't completely beaten. She forced her bruised lips into a charming smile.

'You've talked me into it!'

CHAPTER THREE

DWYNWEN was lying in bed, shrunken and old, and as Owen lowered Lallie to the floor, she realised just how old Dwynwen must be. Seventy, she thought, or perhaps even seventy-five.

She had stifled a gasp of dismay when she had first caught sight of the old lady, but she had painted a smile on her face and kept it going grimly. Dwynwen's high colour was gone, leaving her face pale and waxy, and as for her once plentiful white hair, there wasn't much plenty about it now; Lallie could see the shiny scalp through the strands. And Dwynwen's sturdy form had shrunk, there was hardly a bump in the bedclothes to show where she was lying. For the first time, Lallie felt afraid.

She must have stiffened, because Owen's arm tightened about her in the old familiar, comforting way as it had done when she was a child and a favourite cat or dog had died.

'It's all right, Lallie,' he murmured in her ear in a tone too low and muffled for Dwynwen to hear. 'She's on the mend.' Owen had always been kind to her when she was little, he had seemed to know how she felt then.

'Hello, Dwynny.' Lallie watched the old house-keeper's black eyes lose their opaqueness and become once more sharp.

'Come home, have you? Bad girl!' Dwynwen's

voice had changed as well, it was throaty and she stumbled a bit over the words, but there was a faint tinge of her old vigour still remaining. Lallie slid down on to the unwrinkled coverlet.

'About time,' she teased, while her heart ached. 'I can see you've been pining for me.'

Dwynwen's eyes went to Owen, standing at the foot of the bed. 'You keep her here this time, my lad. We need her.'

'Everything arranged.' He picked up Lallie's left hand and waved it under Dwynwen's nose. 'Shackled!' He sounded triumphant and Lallie awarded him top marks for acting ability, deciding to equal it and if possible, better it.

'Oh, he's arranged it all right,' she grinned. 'He's immobilised me, nearly broken my ankle!'

Dwynwen's eyes closed and then flicked open again. 'Do with a cup of tea,' she muttered. 'That Nerys makes it too weak.'

Lallie flicked her black head at Owen and he left the room, whereat she chuckled.

'Obedient, isn't he?'

The ghost of a smile touched the housekeeper's mouth. 'Always are,' and her eyelid drooped in a travesty of a wink. 'When they're getting their own way.' She struggled a brown, workworn claw out from under the bedclothes and grasped Lallie's wrist. 'Stay here with us, *cariad*, this is your place.'

At any other time, Lallie would have denied it hotly. This wasn't her place, she was a stranger, despite all the years she'd lived here. She was just a stray they'd taken in and made welcome for the sake of her mother, she didn't really belong, not like

Owen, Jonty and Dorcas. But now she meekly bowed her head and laid her hand on the frail old brown one.

After all, she and Dwynwen were really in the same position, they neither of them belonged, not properly, and Dwynwen must have felt this even more than she had done herself, otherwise the old lady would never have worried so much about her future when she was too old to work any longer. To Lallie, being sent away had been a grief, but it hadn't been the end of the world, she had been young and resilient but that sort of threat hanging over Dwynwen's head, it must have been terrifying.

Behind her smile, she worked it all out, surprised she'd never thought of it this way before. To her, Dwynwen had been a permanent part of the scenery, a fixture like a brick in the wall—to be there till the house crumbled away. She had based this supposition on the fact that in some tenuous fashion, Dwynny and Owen were related. She recalled Dwynwen talking about it, about her grandmother and great-grandfather who had been Tudors, and Lallie, without any living relatives, had made more of this than she should have done.

She had believed firmly in family ties, but apparently Dwynwen wasn't so sure of their strength and endurance. All the same, Dwynny should have known that Owen would never send her away from this house. Hadn't he built on this extension purposely—a bedroom, sitting room and bathroom, so that the old lady would no longer have to climb stairs, and hadn't he decreed there would be no big evening meal—that they should have dinner at mid-

day so that the housekeeper should have the afternoons and evenings to herself?

No, she was sure of it, this had nothing to do with
Owen, he probably hadn't known anything about it,
but—and here Lallie's eyes glowed venomously—
he'd imported the person who had dropped the
poison, and surely that person wouldn't have said
anything without first having been given some en-
couragement to think herself in a position to do so.

So it *was* Owen's fault, and that was another black
mark against him. Damn him and his tomcatting
tendencies! It wasn't so bad when he kept them
separate—when he confined them to the occasional
weekend away. He'd no right to bring them home!

As if she'd conjured him up just by thinking about
him, he came in with the tea tray. Dwynwen drank
her tea, but when Lallie rose to go, she found her
hand imprisoned in the old lady's. 'You'll stay,
Lallie, promise?'

'I've no option.' Lallie put on a cheerful front.
'Owen's been laying down the law ever since he
found me in London, but it's not only that. I was
getting a bit fed up anyway. Spring's coming and I
wanted to be here to see it.'

'Getting married?' Dwynwen touched the ring
and looked up, almost slyly.

'Of course!' That was Owen being firm and giving
Lallie no chance of spoiling things. 'But not for a
while yet, we can't have a wedding without you, old
girl so you'd better pull yourself together and start
getting well fast. I can't wait for ever.'

'There was no need for you to be so damn coy with

Dwynwen!' Lallie brought it out ferociously as they were sitting at supper. She helped herself to another slice of cold ham—a large one—anointed it with mustard and pickles and reached for another slice of bread and butter.

Owen raised his eyebrows, smoothing back the lock of russet hair which always dropped over his forehead. 'She likes it. It's what she expects—the sly glance, the innuendo, it's meat and drink to her.' He fetched himself another can of lager from the fridge, pouring some into his glass and shaking the tin at her. 'There's some left, want it?'

At the shake of her head, he resumed pouring into his own glass. 'And you, my little pet, are supposed to blush with shy, maidenly modesty, but I won't demand the impossible from you. What was he like, your ageing Romeo? Did he make your flinty heart go pit-a-pat?'

Lallie choked on a mouthful and reached for the teapot. 'No, he didn't,' she said furiously when she had her breath back. 'I've told you and told you, there was nothing! I'll repeat it if you like, *nothing*! We've had all this out before, and I'd like it if you never mentioned the subject again. You didn't believe me then and you're not believing me now, so what's the point?' She poured her tea with a shaking hand. 'You obviously believe it, so it must be true, anything you believe is always the truth. Or is it that you *need* to believe it—that it brings me down to your level? If that's the case, I don't need to worry overmuch. If I tried for years, I'd never get down to where you are.' She took a gulp from her cup and shuddered at the sweetness. 'Owen, please listen to me. This is an impossible situation, you must see that. I can't live like this, not even for a few months.'

'Then stop pretending, Lallie. Try being honest for a change, you'll find it a great relief.'

She threw down her knife and fork and rose from the table swiftly, wincing a little as she knocked her ankle against the table leg. 'You want honesty, I've given it to you, but you weren't satisfied—it wasn't a good enough story—well, have the other one which I shall fabricate for you on the spot. My ageing Romeo was very nice, very kind and very considerate, and as well as him, there've been at least six others, all old men. I have a yen for them. Do you like that story any better?'

'You little tramp!' He sprang to his feet and towered over her, his eyes blazing.

'See what I mean?' She faced him and her face was a small, white mask of bitterness. 'You'll believe anything filthy about me, won't you? You want to believe it!' And she limped out of the kitchen and upstairs to her room where she flung herself on the bed. It would have been lovely to be able to cry, but the tears wouldn't come. They stayed—a hard lump in her throat hurting when she took a breath so that she thought she would choke. She heard her bedroom door open and swung round to see Owen.

'Get out!' The words came out as almost a snarl. 'You're too young, Owen, you need another fifteen years to get into my bracket.' Her hand reached for the hairbrush on the dressing table. 'Out!' she repeated. 'I like them old, withered and at least fifty. You don't qualify!'

As she said it, she knew she'd made a mistake. She

should have ignored him completely or kept her temper and said something soft—perhaps she should have cried a bit. But it was too late, the words had been said and she couldn't take them back. They hung in the air like a curtain of stinging things. She raised her hand, gripping the hairbrush defiantly, lifting it above her head, but Owen caught her arm before she had a chance to throw it.

'Don't try me too far, Lallie.' His face, like her own, was white with temper. 'You might make me want to find out for myself, and I don't think you'd like that. I wouldn't be very gentle in my present state of mind. Go to bed before you say another word, and while you're still safe. I came up here to arrange some sort of truce—as you said, this situation's impossible, so I think we should start tomorrow afresh. No yesterdays and no tomorrows—that way, I might keep my sanity and my temper. Will that do you?'

Lallie nodded dumbly and watched him as he went out of the door.

Lallie stood in the kitchen. She wasn't flustered or overcome by the woman who had come in to join her, she was merely filled with a depressing envy. So this was Owen's old school friend, his Mrs Stella Prentice? Lallie thought he should consult the nearest dictionary about the correct meaning of the word 'altruism'. He'd evidently made a mistake in using it, because in this case she didn't think it applied. No wonder he'd gone off early and left her to it!

She had been expecting she didn't quite know what, but certainly nobody like this. Perhaps a faded, rather careworn widow, somebody who looked as though she'd been marked by life, and she couldn't have been more wrong. Stella might have been in school with him, which would make her about thirty-five, but she didn't look a day over thirty—and there was worse to come. She had just the looks which Lallie had always wanted for herself, silver-blonde hair, swept back in sculptured waves into a classical chignon, the type Lallie had always wished for but could never achieve—her own hair was too thick and heavy for it—and Stella had a complexion like a rose petal, several shades lighter than her own rather dark skin.

And Stella was tall and graceful—at least five foot seven and with an adequate amount of all the usual ins and outs. Her bosom was a real bosom, it deserved the word! Lallie's envy grew. There was nothing much the matter with her own, of course, they were there—high and firm but small, all right as long as you didn't mind skimpy things—and Stella's legs, they were beautiful as well, long and slender, ending in long, slender feet. She was all woman and she made Lallie feel like an adolescent school-girl.

Stella was smiling at her, a mistress—hired help smile—beautiful, understanding, firm and ever so slightly condescending.

'Good morning, Lallie, you look just as you've been described to me, Owen has a wonderful gift for verbal sketching, I think I'd have known you any-where. I'm sure we shall get along splendidly.'

'Good morning, Stella.' Apparently Christian names were going to be the order of things and a small fib this early in their acquaintance wouldn't hurt, so she fibbed. 'I'm sure we shall.' But Stella had other ideas.

'Mrs Prentice, dear.' Stella looked rueful and the smile was kept going, although her pale blue eyes had hardened. 'I like to start as I mean to go on and it's better to get these things straight right away. I'm sure you'll understand, but I always insist on formality. You see, I've had quite a bit of experience in the hotel trade and I've always found it pays to insist on formality. You know the saying about familiarity leading to contempt—I assure you it's true, and I've found that a familiar staff is a sloppy staff.' It was quite a long speech, but Stella did it beautifully. Her diction was elegant and precise and although she hadn't lost every bit of her Welsh accent, it came over as a gentle lilt which made her speaking voice very attractive.

Lallie's nostrils thinned and she had to lower her eyes to hide the fighting gleam behind her lashes, while the whole of her body tensed with anger. She wasn't a snob, that sort of thing had never gone down well with the Tudors, they might be farmers and they'd made a lot of money at it, but they never chucked their weight about. So, she was staff, was she—she firmly repressed a desire to go straight up to her room, pack her case and ring for a taxi. The thought of Dwynwen helped in her decision not to budge. She couldn't leave Dwynny to the mercies of this arrogant bitch!

But why hadn't Owen explained to his Stella about the situation? And then she remembered, he'd had no chance. Stella had gone on holiday before

Dwynwen's heart attack, so Stella, only just back from wherever she'd been, would have only the local gossip to rely on. That gossip would have been fairly comprehensive, but not all that reliable, and it wouldn't have contained any details of Owen's 'master plan'; that was a strictly private matter between herself and him.

All this flashed through her brain at the speed of light, together with the comforting thought that six years in London had given her a thin veneer of sophistication behind which she could take shelter. Only it was too thin really, only an eggshell thickness which would shatter at the first knock. So, instead of uttering the first biting words that came to her lips, she choked them back and raised limpid, innocent eyes to Stella, who didn't realise the danger when those eyes turned gold.

'As you wish,' Lallie murmured, 'but I think it's carrying formality a bit far and I don't think Owen would understand. He'd think we didn't get on if he heard me calling you Mrs Prentice. Besides, if I called you that, I'd have to call him Mr Tudor, and I don't think I could be that formal with a man who used to bath me when I was little. But if you want to call me Miss Moncke, I shan't mind in the least, although I'd still think it was ridiculous. This isn't a hotel and I'm not exactly staff—I'm Lallie, come to take over until Dwynwen's well and able to cope once more.'

All through this, Stella kept her smile going and Lallie gave her top marks for a more than adequate layer of sophistication; she even envied that as well.

'Ah yes,' Stella allowed herself to be diverted, it

was easier than squabbling about what they should call each other. 'How is Dwynwen?'

'On the mend.' It was Owen's phrase and Lallie echoed it, adding her own comment as an after thought. 'Sitting up and taking nourishment—and now, if you'll excuse me . . .' she nodded to where a lump of dough was sitting on the floured board, ready to be rolled out, 'I have to get on with dinner or we'll be having it at teatime.'

'Dinner.' Stella became businesslike and judicious. 'Now that's one thing I'd like you to change, and as soon as possible. I'm sure it would be no trouble to you and so much better for Owen. It would be much better to have the main meal in the evening, don't you think? About half past seven would be a very good time. Owen's so rarely here for a meal at midday and it would give you more time to get on with your household chores.'

Lallie dropped her meekness like an outworn cloak and with it went any intention of trying to preserve the mistress/staff relationship which Stella was trying to establish. 'Not on your life!' she wagged her head firmly. 'I'm not slaving over a hot stove all evening or spending half the night washing up. Breakfast's at seven-thirty, dinner's at one, tea is at five and there's a cold supper laid out any time after nine-thirty. It's all part of Owen's Law, he fixed it that way, and that's the way I like it.'

'But Owen's so rarely here for dinner.' Stella was gentle but firm.

'That's his fault,' Lallie marched to the table, shook some flour on to the rolling pin and raised it defiantly. 'He brought me back here to run things and I'd prefer not to make any changes. When Dwynwen's well enough to run things once more, she'll find everything as it always was. She's not a young woman, you know, she has her ways and she likes to stick to them.'

'A very inflexible attitude,' Stella murmured. 'I've noticed, though, that it's generally like that with the older people. I've usually found that when a person refuses to change a routine because "they've always done it that way", it's time he or she was retired, and really, the question is—will Dwynwen ever be fit again to take over the running of this house?'

Lallie shrugged. 'Who knows? I certainly hope so, but even if she can never "do" again, she can always keep an eye on things, supervise and feel useful. I don't know how it's happened, but from somewhere, she's had this idea that Owen was going to put her in a home for the aged. It's taken us ages, both of us, to convince her that it's not true. Changing a routine as you suggest would just wake all her worries again, besides being inconvenient for me. I'm used to a nine-till-five job, I like my evenings free.' And she started to roll out her pastry industriously, feeling evil and angry.

Stella sighed in a resigned way as though she was having trouble with a particularly obdurate 'staff'. 'I'm going into the office,' she said as she went to the door. 'Send the girl in with my coffee at eleven.'

Lallie rolled steadily and raised her eyes. 'Nerys is doing the bedrooms this morning, Stella,' she nodded at the open door through which came the whine of the vacuum cleaner and the stump of Nerys' heavy feet. 'I'm afraid she won't have time, but coffee will be in here, in the kitchen at eleven, if you want it,' and she watched the pale grey pleated skirt flirt about the slender legs as Stella went off to the office.

She left the door open and through it, after a lot of drawer and file cabinet banging, she heard the hesitant tap of a typewriter in inexperienced hands, and chuckled softly to herself as she thought about the report to the Milk Marketing Board. Owen had shown it to her the previous evening when he had finished writing it and he had pointed out the format, the underlining of the paragraph headings and the two whole pages of statistics which were to accompany it. He had then dropped it in her lap where she sat curled up on the couch, with a bland, 'I'll leave it with you, Lallie. I'd like it as soon as possible'. She gave another nasty smile. He'd get it when his Stella had finished it, and that sounded like a couple of days from where she was standing. He'd wait for it, and good luck to him!

At half past ten, the doctor arrived to see Dwynwen and the old housekeeper, washed, brushed and with a pink bedjacket modestly covering the informality of her white flannelette nightgown and with her hair in a neat plait, received him and submitted to his sphygmomanometer and stethoscope with ill-concealed irritation. Lallie, who had done the washing, brushing and the neatening of the already spotless bedroom, stood at the bottom of the bed and pinned a bright, encouraging smile on her face to cover her concern. The smile vanished when, the examination over, she walked back to the kitchen with the doctor.

'She'll be all right, won't she? Please tell me the

truth.' She spoke with the informality of long acquaintance. This was the man who had attended her
through half a dozen childhood ailments.

'Yes, Lallie, she'll be all right, so don't look so
worried.' He patted her head as though she was once
more a child and she was tempted to bite the hand
that patted. 'But it will be a long job and you mustn't
expect too much.' He smiled down at her, and then
his eyes went to the table where the mugs were set
ready for coffee and where Stella was sitting, fingers
and one shoe tapping with impatience. Lallie, intent
on Dwynwen, didn't even notice her there. Her eyes
were fixed on the doctor's face as if she might find the
truth in his features, but there was nothing to be read
there, not any more than he'd said, so she lifted the
coffee pot from the counter and waved it under his
nose.

'Want some?'

'When did I ever say no?' and he sat down at the
table as Lallie put the pot down where everybody
could help themselves. By this time she had seen
Stella, but Stella was only a minor consideration; at
this moment, all her thoughts were concentrated on
Dwynwen.

'Tell me about it,' she demanded. 'How long, and
will she ever be completely well again?'

'Six months—a year perhaps, but no, Lallie,' he
looked at her with pity, 'she won't ever be completely
right, but she has a lot of years in her yet and with the
proper care . . . We'll keep her blood pressure down
with tablets and she's lost a lot of that excess weight
she was carrying, which is a big help, and later on, in
about a month's time, she should start getting about

a bit, but anything strenuous would be out of the question, of course. You'll be able to cope, though, and I'll see you have help with the nursing, somebody to come in and bath her, give her a bit of massage and so on, and later on, I'll send her up a walking aid.' He patted Lallie's hand again. 'No, don't look so gloomy—she's very lucky, that place Owen built on for her is ideal, no steps or stairs. Meanwhile, keep her happy and you can start her on a more substantial diet from now on.'

Lallie glanced at the oven. 'Steak pie?' she queried, and at his nod, 'Good, there won't be a cloud in her sky, I promise you that.' As she said it, she knew she was promising away part of her life, but it didn't matter. She tossed her job, her flat and her cherished independence into a mental dustbin, meanwhile assuring herself that she could cope with Owen if she had to. He could think and say what he liked about her, that didn't matter either. She wouldn't pay any more attention to his little digs, she'd let them go straight over her head. If he wanted to think her every sort of a trollop, so what? Everybody was entitled to their own opinions. She wasn't a trollop, she knew it, and that should be good enough.

The doctor drained his mug, smacked his lips and with a valedictory 'See she keeps taking the tablets', he let himself out, leaving Stella and Lallie together in the kitchen.

'Don't you think it would be better for all concerned if she went into a home where she'd get the proper attention?' Stella sounded weary of the whole thing as though everybody was making too much fuss about it. 'I know it's hard to get a place in one nowadays, but I'm sure Owen could use a bit of influence . . .'

Lallie had moved over to the oven and she raised a flushed but otherwise serene face from her inspection of the steak pies and apple tarts. 'This *is* her home, Stella,' she said quietly and in a voice which brooked no argument. 'It's been her home ever since Owen's mother died when Dorcas was born, and it always will be her home. Please don't ever mention this again, not to me, and certainly not to Dwynwen. Oh!' She tilted her head as she heard footsteps in the passage. 'That sounds like Owen, he's early,' she marvelled. 'I wonder if he met the doctor on the way up?'

Owen pushed the door open and came in, big, rainspattered and smiling. His greeting, 'Hello Stella, had a good time?' was brief, he didn't even wait for an answer. He concentrated on Lallie.

'Can you have dinner ready by twelve-thirty, *cariad?* I have to go to Lampeter this afternoon,' and he came round the table to stand over her.

'You're looking very pleased with life.' Lallie's eyes met his gravely. 'Did you meet the doctor?—he's only just left.'

'No.' He looked down at her and there was a message in his sherry brown eyes, but she ignored it, blinking at him like a cat. 'It's spring,' he murmured, 'and in the spring, it's said a young man's fancy lightly turns . . .' He put a delicate, hardly noticeable emphasis on the word 'young'.

'But the operative word is "lightly", isn't it?' She gave him a sugary smile of welcome. 'And who are you fancying so lightly in Lampeter?' She raised one eyebrow in almost exact immitation of his own and her smile grew, if anything, sweeter.

'Not in Lampeter, nearer home.' He put a hand on each of her shoulders, holding her firmly where she was. 'Don't be so shy, Lallie, Stella will look the other way,' and calmly, deliberately he claimed her mouth with his own. When he raised his head, Lallie took a deep breath and tried to look nonchalant; it was the hardest thing she'd ever done. She'd braved newspaper reporters and their cameramen, she'd even read the slime they'd written about her in the papers and come up smiling, but this was too much!

Owen had turned on all his know-how, all his expertise. He'd scattered her wits and set her trembling, while deep in the pit of her stomach, something hot and sweet had stirred into life, and he'd done it carelessly and with as little effort as he would have used to light a cigarette. Lallie had heard girls speak about being turned on and this, she supposed, was what they meant. He'd kissed her and he'd forced her to respond to him, so that now her lips were quivering, wanting more. It made her angry with him and with herself and her eyes sparked dangerously.

'Damn you, Owen!' she hissed as out of the corner of her eye she saw Stella's departure. Stella had got the message as Owen had intended she should, and that was what it had all been about. He hadn't the courage to say, 'Look, Stella, you're wasting your time'—to be honest and direct about it; he'd used her, Lallie, to get the message over, and he'd not been delicate about it, he'd done it with a sledgehammer. She wrenched herself away from his hands.

'Do you have to be so—so cruel about it?' she hissed. 'Damn you again, I won't be used like that!'

'You'll be used any way I choose.' Now that they were alone, he dropped his bantering tone. 'And don't look so outraged—you liked it! Have you been starving yourself lately?—your mouth felt very hungry.'

'I'm on a strict diet,' she snarled back at him. 'Too many's too tiring and I have to think of my health. Now, if you want an early dinner, go and take your kisses where they're welcome.'

'They're welcome right here,' and he smiled at her in open triumph. 'Besides, to whom else should I give them but to my loving little affianced wife? Now I'm engaged, I shouldn't play the field any more and you shouldn't encourage me to. Come on, Lallie, remember what I said about honesty—you liked it.'

'All right!' She stepped back from him and looked him squarely in the eyes. 'You want honesty, you'll get it. I'm human, the same as other people, I'm twenty-six, and when a personable man kisses me, it's perfectly natural I should feel some response. I expect, if I gave you the opportunity, you could make me want you, but that's all you can make me do!'

'Correction, Lallie. If your hungry little mouth is anything to go by, I can make you do anything I want.' Abruptly, he left the subject. 'By the way, I dropped a notice of our engagement into the offices of the local rag this morning, it'll be in tomorrow's edition which comes out late in the afternoon, so as it's Monday today, you can expect Jonty and his girl-friend over on Wednesday or Thursday. I haven't told him you're back here yet, otherwise he'd have been beating a path to the door before now.'

'Coming here!' Lallie's attention was diverted. 'But you said Dwynwen . . .'

'What the eye doesn't see . . .' he chuckled. 'Dwynwen's in her own place and if you put tea or whatever it is in the front parlour . . . There's no need to tell her and get her worked up into a state, she mustn't be upset, we don't want a relapse. And you can tell me what *you* think of the young lady. I've a few reservations myself, I'd be glad of your opinion. What did the doctor say about the old girl?'

'Quiet, rest, no worries.' Lallie made the report terse while trying not to miss out on anything. 'He said she could go on a more substantial diet—six months to a year before she's able to get about much, but she'll never be completely fit again.' There was sadness in her face and in the despondent droop of her shoulders. All the fight had gone out of her, leaving her limp and defenceless.

'We'll take care of her, *cariad*.' Owen's arm was about her waist gently urging her against him and his tone was the one he used to sick animals, kind, soothing and comforting, so that she turned into his arm, letting go of her hard-held control and forgetting temporarily the insults they hurled at each other, while her head dropped on to his chest and her eyes filled with tears.

'Shush, girl!' She felt him stroke her head, much as he'd done when she was a small child.

'He said she'd got a lot of years left in her,' she sobbed into his shirt front, and then tore herself out of his arm to turn her back on him and blow her nose vigorously. 'Damn, damn, *damn*! I'm getting sentimental,' she exploded. 'If you want an early meal, go and wash. It'll be on the table when you're ready—and call Nerys on the way down or she'll be stuck up there with that vacuum cleaner till the cows come home!'

CHAPTER FOUR

FOUR days had gone by, days in which Lallie could have been supremely happy if it hadn't been for the battle between herself and Owen. She had mastered the peculiarities of the solid fuel cooker, Dwynwen was steadily improving, she was now at the stage where she was critical of the cooking, and Stella hadn't been too bad either.

Stella didn't accept the situation, she ignored it—treating the ruby ring and the notice in the paper as a sort of sick joke, a minor problem which would go away if she took no notice of it, but on the other hand, she had concentrated on her work and left the running of the household strictly to Lallie, for which Lallie was suitably grateful.

It wasn't so much a battle between her and Owen as a series of skirmishes which started at the oddest times—they came out of a clear blue sky. One moment, they were talking sensibly—they were even cautiously friendly, and the next, they were exchanging insults. One such exchange had just taken place. Lallie, in the middle of preparing breakfast, had gone to answer the phone, swearing under her breath at having to leave bacon sizzling in the pan, but the phone was generally busy between seven in the morning and nine, after which she could ignore its demanding ring, since Stella was there to answer it.

It had been Jonty, and she was just getting into her

stride when Owen had come down the stairs for breakfast, looking his usual well dressed and immaculate self even in hairy lovat tweeds. That had been when he said 'Jonty?' with a raised eyebrow, and at her nod, 'then hang up, darling, I want my breakfast, I've got a busy day.'

Wrath had exploded in her and she had yelled down the phone, 'Did you hear that, Jonty? The great man has spoken! Are you going to come over to see us? Oh, there's no privacy . . .' as Owen had tilted the phone to share the earpiece.

'The day after tomorrow,' Jonty had said laconically.

'*And* your shepherdess,' Lallie had insisted.

'Never go anywhere without her,' and Owen had taken the phone from her.

'Come for tea and stay for supper,' he'd suggested, and hung up.

'That was a bit curt,' Lallie had expostulated. 'We were half way through a very interesting conversation.'

'The phone's mainly for business,' he snapped as he sat down at the table and picked up the teapot. 'I have to keep in touch with the office and since old Meredith's gone sick, I have to see to the practice in Trellwyd. The new man's all right, but he can't be out on a visit and take calls at the same time. What did Jonty have to say, anyway?'

'Congratulations mainly,' she said waspishly. 'And explanations for the delay, of course. Apparently his shepherdess doesn't read the local paper, she only makes the fire with it, and Jonty's been busy with the lambing so they didn't know about this farcical engagement until yesterday when he called into the post office and Nerys' mother gave him the news.'

She recalled Jonty's voice, a bit wry as he said, 'I always knew you and Owen would . . .' and she had been going to deny anything of the sort when Owen had come interrupting. 'There's lots I wanted to ask,' she muttered as she slid the bacon and eggs on to his plate.

'Ask them when they come.' He was unmoved.

'And there's something I have to ask you now.' She poured a cup of tea for herself, added milk and sugar and stirred while she thought of the best way to make the request. Owen didn't seem to be in a good mood, although that wasn't unexpected. There was no audience this morning, so he didn't have to put on a show.

'I want to borrow the Land Rover,' she said baldly, and at his look of surprised amusement: 'It's all very well for you, you've got all your bits and pieces here, but you dragged me away without giving me much time and you never mentioned anything as long as six months, did you? I just flung a few things in a case, enough for a few days . . .'

'Don't say any more,' he sighed. 'Somebody's coming to tea and you haven't a thing to wear. But no dice, little one, you're not borrowing any vehicle of mine. You're lethal on a bicycle!' and as she began to protest, 'You had an endorsement on your licence a month after you passed the test. Speeding, wasn't it?' He pushed his plate aside and refilled his cup. 'Have you done any driving since you've been in London?'

'No,' she muttered. 'How could I? I didn't have a car.'

'And you couldn't hire one, not with an endorsement. I think that says it all—the hire car firms wouldn't trust you, so why should I? Tell me where you want to go and I'll drive you.'

'This afternoon?' and at his nod, 'Aber, please, and we'll have a truce for the rest of the day, no nasty remarks.'

'A truce?' Owen raised his head and looked at her as though he didn't believe his ears. 'We've tried that, if you remember. We've done nothing but have truces since you arrived here, and they don't seem to work. I thought we'd arranged it, there were to be no yesterdays and no tomorrows, but you somehow can't get the yesterdays out of your mind, you keep dragging them up for an airing.'

'Me?' she exclaimed indignantly, her voice rising in a scolding tone. 'I'm not to blame, it's you who goes on and on . . .'

'There, see what happens!' Owen pushed the teacup aside and reached for his pipe. 'Instead of being civilised, behaving like an ordinary human being, you go up in the air again—you've got a defence mechanism second to none.'

'Don't bother,' she flared. 'I can manage without your help. I'll make do with what I have, don't put yourself out for me!' The flare died away and she became calm. 'Now let me see, which would you prefer, jeans and a sweater? They're always acceptable, aren't they?—or I could use the remaining things from my case, like four pairs of tights, some bras, a load of panties and a clean nightie—oh, and I forgot, I found a couple of my old school dresses, I could wear one of those, if you don't mind it open down the front and a bit wrinkled over my rear. It's a bit mini as well, I should look devastating!'

'You're being deliberately obstructive,' he accused.

'The man has a mind like a needle,' she marvelled. 'I require transport to Aber, but I'm not accepting your offer unless you cut out the nasty bits like reminding me about doing forty miles an hour in a thirty-mile limit and then saying I'm not fit to drive. I'll ring Jonty and ask him, he'd do a favour for me, I daresay.'

'I've told you, I'll take you. Be ready when you've given Dwynwen her dinner.'

'And no nasty bits, everything to be sweetness and light for the trip?' and at his nod, 'A magnificent gesture, dear Owen. What payment do you expect?'

Suddenly he grinned wickedly at her. 'You ask that? Come on, Lallie, you know the ropes—I'll expect very much the same as your old men received.'

She looked down at her plate, thinking that all the fun had gone out of crossing swords with him again, but that was because, to her, it was a kind of game, whereas to him it was in deadly earnest.

'That's the worst of young men,' she sighed when she had recovered herself. 'They're so physical, they wear a girl out. Come to me when you're in the sere and yellow, the withered leaf, and I'll give you a nice kiss and a cuddle.'

'Strumpet!' But he was laughing as he said it.

Dwynwen looked at Lallie over the tray containing her dinner, her eyes taking in tights, high-heeled shoes, the slim, pleated grey skirt and clean sweater. 'You going out?'

'Mmm, shopping. Nerys is going to stay with you until I get back—she's full of gossip today, she said two whole sentences one after the other this morning, so you'll be able to have a nice chat.'

'Where's your coat?' Dwynwen's eyes were sharp. 'Can't go out in this cold wind without one, it's only March.'

'Didn't bring one,' Lallie said cheerfully, 'but not to worry. There's an old anorak of Jonty's in the hall, I'll borrow that.'

'Your mam's coat's upstairs in the big bedroom.' The old lady dug her spoon into the small heap of mashed potatoes, nudged a little minced beef on to the spoonful and conveyed it carefully to her mouth. 'Nice,' she murmured when she had swallowed it. 'Should fit you, your mam was only little, like you.'

'Mothballs,' Lallie shook her head, 'it's been up there for twelve years.'

'No mothballs,' Dwynwen contradicted indignantly. 'Soap in the pockets.' She went on eating, slow spoonful by slow spoonful, until the plate was empty. 'And a nice cup of tea before you go,' she added sternly.

Lallie went back to the kitchen where Owen and Stella were still eating and began to ladle trifle into glass dishes. 'Dwynny suggests I should borrow a coat of my mother's, she says there's one upstairs with the pockets full of soap.' She looked at Owen with a melting glance, full of humility. 'Is that all right with you?'

'Of course, darling,' Owen reciprocated, laying it on with a trowel so that Lallie glared at him behind Stella's back. 'There are a few other things, if you want them,' he continued blandly. 'Some bits of jewellery and a string of pearls. I'll get them out of the safe for you this evening.'

'And what do I have to do for that?' She mouthed the words at him silently and flushed as he looked at her, letting his eyes slide over her insolently. He made no attempt to disguise his meaning and she felt a peculiar sensation beginning in the pit of her stomach, and then, at his knowledgeable smile, she blinked and looked the other way, her thoughts in a turmoil. It was her own fault, she'd deliberately encouraged him to think the worst of her, so she had only herself to blame, but it wasn't fair. He was using all his considerable know-how and she couldn't cope with it.

Several stinging phrases occurred to her, but she dismissed them. They'd only spark off another row, and that she could do without, so she decided to play his game. She'd never win, she knew, but surely Owen couldn't do anything or say anything much with Stella sitting opposite him at the table. She sidled up to him and put a hand on his hair.

'You're so good to me, Owen,' she murmured throatily in a loving tone. 'My lovely, lovely ring, now more jewellery and some pearls—I'll have to think of something—some wonderful treat to repay you for all this kindness.'

'Easy.' He dropped his fork and his arm slid round her waist, squeezing cruelly. 'You can finish off the

Milk Marketing Board report tonight, when we get back. Stella's having the afternoon off.'

It was cold in Aber, the wind was blowing strongly straight off the grey, stormy waters of Cardigan Bay and whistling down the main street of the little town. There was no escape from it, and Lallie was glad of her mother's coat, which was a lot more luxurious than she had supposed, a soft, silky musquash which fitted her perfectly and didn't look as though it had hung in a wardrobe for twelve years. She huddled into it gratefully.

'I don't remember this coat,' she told him.

'Why should you?' He was flattening. 'You were only about thirteen the last time you saw it and you were far more interested in getting the better of me, weren't you? I think you devoted every waking moment to defying me. You were a pest!'

'Thanks,' she said briefly, and trotted at his side while she examined price labels in shop windows with a jaundiced eye.

'Everything's twice as expensive here as it should be,' she scolded. 'I'd get things much cheaper in London or even in Newtown.'

'Trying to impress me with your sense of economy?' Owen's fingers were hard about her elbow. 'Don't waste your time and mine, I know you too well. To the cost of whatever you bought in Newtown, we'd have to add the cost of the petrol to get there, and the Bentley drinks like a fish! You can find what you want here, surely—there are some very good shops, this is quite a high-class resort, so try this one.' And he pushed her through the doors of a large store.

Lallie wasn't trying to impress, she was doing rapid calculations in her head—and she wasn't too happy with the result. Oh well—she put her Greek holiday into a mental dustbin and decided she'd have to spend the money which she'd saved so carefully for the past six months. There wouldn't be any comforting pay cheque at the end of March to rely on and Owen hadn't mentioned money in his arbitrary arrangements.

Beguiled by the warmth, she plunged into a very controlled orgy of spending. Her cheque book was in her bag and she knew to a penny how much she could afford, and if Owen offered her anything at the end of her stay here—her eyes brightened—he could take his magnanimity and choke on it!

Her purchases completed, she drew out her cheque book, but he reached over her to take the bill and scowl at it, a sum which, to her, represented a sizeable slice out of a whole month's salary.

'Is it enough?' His eyes ran down the list of purchases and the line of his mouth hardened.

'Oh yes,' she said emphatically. 'I've kept it small—well, smallish because I want some shoes as well. I'm trying to be economical,' she exploded, 'and when you look like that, I can see I shan't get much help from you. Kindly remember, I'm a working girl, not a wealthy farmer, and,' her voice dropped to a low mutter, 'this coat doesn't help any. That salesgirl thinks I'm loaded!'

'These are false economy,' Owen pointed out several items. 'Why buy manmade fibres when you can have good wool?'

'They're easier to wash,' she hissed, while out of

the corner of her eye she could see the assistant pulling out trays of cashmere twinsets, the ones at which she had already shaken her head and refused to contemplate. Owen examined them seriously, his long fingers feeling the softness.

'These, I think,' he indicated a rose pink and a soft gold, then he made out his own cheque for the total amount with a casual, 'We'll collect later,' before he hauled Lallie out into the street to head for a nearby teashop.

'If I was bigger and stronger, I'd wring your neck,' Lallie muttered it to him as he pushed her into a seat. 'And don't think you're getting away with it! I was quite happy with what I'd chosen and the things were what I could afford. I can't afford cashmere twinsets, and they're not very practical anyway, they have to be cleaned. And I'm not going to earn them in the way you suggested—I'm referring to that dirty glance you gave me at the dinner table. I'll pay you for the other things, but I'm certainly not paying you for your little extras. You can give them to one of your women!'

'Don't be vulgar,' she was told in a repressive voice. 'Consider them as a gift, with no strings attached—manmade fibres are going to be the ruin of sheep farmers. In any case,' his eyes slid over her mockingly, 'they wouldn't fit what you refer to as "my women". All of them have considerably more . . .' He looked pointedly at her slender figure and Lallie went quiet. She should have known better than to start anything with Owen in a public place. 'Stop being a contrary brat,' he advised. 'There's no need for you to pay me for anything, have the lot as a gift.'

'I don't think I'd care for the pay-off,' she shot back at him. 'What had you in mind, a quiet week-end at a discreet hotel upcountry?'

'Eight years away *has* broadened your mind!' He watched her lazily as she poured tea. 'Have a toasted teacake and give your mouth something else to do but spit out your nasty little thoughts about my private life.'

'You didn't hesitate to tell me what you thought of mine,' she reminded him.

'But I was acting *in loco parentis*,' he pointed out. 'Remember, Lallie, your mother left you in my care. It was my business to pry.'

'Not the way you did,' she muttered defiantly. 'I never slated you for doing improper things—and heaven knows, you've done enough of them. Compared with you, I'm the original Snow White. In any case, you jumped to conclusions, which just shows how bad your mind is.'

'No yesterdays,' he reminded her. 'That was what we agreed, wasn't it? So why d'you have to keep raking them up.' He stirred his tea reflectively and pushed the plate of teacakes across to her. 'We agreed we'd both stop vilifying each other but you can't leave well alone, can you? Everytime you open your mouth, it's another spiteful jab. It's almost as though you're afraid of something, not me. I bet— Are you afraid of yourself, Lallie?'

She swallowed hard on the little knot of fear which had crept into her throat, and when it was choked down, she gave a jeering little laugh. 'Afraid of you, Owen? Never on this green earth!'

'Which wasn't the question,' he pointed out gravely. 'You've avoided that, so I'll tell you now, you should be afraid of me, my girl. Despite your protestations, I think I could have you any time I wanted, you're a long way from being the cool, remote little thing you pretend.' He looked up quickly and caught her gaze before she could lower her eyes, holding it so that she was fascinated by what she thought were yellow flames flickering behind the sherry brown. She was aware of dry lips, and with an enormous effort she picked up her cup and raised it to her mouth, gulping at it thirstily.

'Bighead,' she jeered softly when she judged her voice would be normal and not a croak. 'Don't waste your time with me, I'm not in your league, and you wouldn't be satisfied with a pushover.'

'Then come along.' He tossed some money down on the table. 'We'll buy Dwynwen a present while we're here, let her know she isn't forgotten. She'll never forgive us if we don't take her something.' The Welsh lilt was coming over strongly in his voice. 'Raisin toffee, *cariad*? She's very fond of that.'

Lallie snorted. 'She's not up to toffee yet. Try some Turkish Delight, she always adored that at Christmas.'

'Mmm,' Owen tucked her hand under his arm as they left the tea-shop, 'and a new handbag to put it in. Something she can show off when she's better and can get down to chapel. Meanwhile she can put it at the bottom of the bed or on the dressing table and crow about it when friends come visiting.'

'That's a nice idea.' Lallie forgot her belligerence. 'A good, big one, something she can swank about.' And for nearly an hour, peace reigned between them as they turned over the contents of a leather shop to find something impressive enough to command respect from any sick visitor. Lallie let Owen pay for it, it was far too expensive for her to even contemplate—as she pointed out, she might have been able to buy the handle, but she had big, gilt initials put on the corner and added a bottle of lavender water and a box of Turkish Delight to go inside.

'You can be a nice little thing when you like, Lallie.' Owen slanted a glance at her as they drove back to Bryn Celyn. 'Why can't you like a little more often?'

'Because I'm what you called me, a contrary brat!' Then her sense of humour peeped out momentarily. 'It's the Anglo-Saxon in me,' she explained demurely. 'We Anglo-Saxons aren't like you Welsh. You tell us we *must* do something and immediately we're looking for ways and means *not* to do it.'

'Tell me something I don't know,' Owen retorted scornfully. 'To be quite honest, I'd worked that out years ago, and the knowledge has come in pretty useful at one time and another.'

'How?' Lallie wrinkled her brow and then gave up. 'Don't count on it any more, though,' she said darkly. 'Think how embarrassing it could be if it recoiled on you!'

That evening, she occupied herself with the remainder of the M.M.B. report and then, when it was finished, she crept into Dwynwen's quarters with a cup of tea for the old lady.

'It's not good for you,' she tried to be severe. 'A milky drink would be much better, it would help you to sleep.'

'Don't want to sleep.' Dwynwen was unrepentant as she sipped at her tea. 'Lots to think about, and all of it good.' She slid a glance to her new bag in pride of place on the dressing table. 'Owen's a good lad, you mind that, wench. *She*'s got her eye on him, and that ring you're wearing won't stop her. Never mind, there's not much longer for her here, soon be April and she'll be off to her hotel—opening for Easter, she said. Pity her poor guests—bread and scrape, that's her—can't save on food and have it tasting right.'

'Wicked old lady,' Lallie reproved, then soothed as she took the empty cup, 'Off to sleep with you, you're looking a lot better,' and she dimmed the light as she went out and softly upstairs to bed.

But Dwynny was quite right about Stella's perseverence in the face of what, to any other woman, would have seemed insuperable odds. Stella wasn't dismayed about the engagement, she seemed to find it amusing, and the looks she had given Lallie during the morning had been tinged with pity. They had made Lallie suspicious so that she had half a mind to tackle Owen about it, but she dismissed the problem as she scrambled into her high, old-fashioned bed, drifting off to sleep almost immediately.

At half past two on the afternoon of Jonty's visit, Lallie came carefully downstairs. Carefully because she was wearing her new pair of very high-heeled black patent court shoes and the thin leather soles had the shine of newness still on them, but she was pleased with them. If there was one part of her anatomy about which she had no worries, it was her legs. For her height, they were long, slender and well shaped, and just at this moment, she thought they were looking their best. Flat heels would have spoiled the effect.

Her black coronet of hair had been brushed until it was smooth and glossy, her face was nicely made up with special attention to her eyes and a new, black pleated skirt swung gently about her legs. She had debated about the cashmere and then, with a shrug, had opened the cellophane packet containing the pink. Owen had said they wouldn't fit any of his bits of fluff and it would be a pity to waste them.

At the bottom of the stairs, she halted while she peered at herself in the wall mirror, a finger going up to smooth her arched brows. The pink colour did things for her, it flattered her slightly sallow complexion and it tended to hide what she had always thought of as a meagre bosom. The soft stuff hinted that there was something there without clinging and emphasising the lack of quantity. In fact there was only one fly in her particular pot of ointment, and she cocked her head to listen to it—the slow, unrhythmic tap of the typewriter from the office, which meant that Stella would have to be invited to the party.

It was sheer curiosity on Stella's part, Lallie knew that, and she also knew that the curiosity had nothing to do with her personally. Stella was anxious to meet Jonty's shepherdess, as was every other woman in the area. He'd been keeping the girl under wraps, hardly anybody had seen her except from a distance. A twinge shot through her ankle, but she dismissed it without giving it any more thought than that it was perfectly healed, the swelling was gone and provided she didn't dash about like a mad thing in these new shoes, she should last out the rest of the day. Owen had been warning her of the dangers of re-straining it which could lead to a permanent weakness.

He came out of the office silently and caught her in her self-congratulatory mood.

'What a ladylike, well-behaved little thing you look, my sweet. Butter wouldn't melt in your mouth, would it?' His eyes slid over her slowly from the crown of her head downwards, then stopped abruptly at her feet. 'What are you wearing those damn fool shoes for? I told you to buy something sensible.'

Lallie raised a supercilious eyebrow, checked the seams of her one and only pair of pure silk stockings and brushed a minute speck from the vamp of her right shoe while she considered her reply. Jonty and his shepherdess would be here very shortly—she didn't want them barging into the middle of a stand-up fight, so a soft answer was the thing—soft enough to turn away wrath.

'I'm walking in them,' she said demurely and then, 'Oh, Owen, I want to look right, and flat shoes would spoil the effect. As you said at the time, it was only a very little sprain, it doesn't hurt at all now.'

'All this for Jonty?' He looked enigmatic. 'Anybody would think he was something special, instead of a fellow you've known most of your life.'

'It's for the shepherdess.' She summoned up a soulful smile. 'It's my own private defence mechanism, the high heels and the hair. They make me look taller, which helps my inferiority complex. Basically, I'm very insecure.'

Owen let out a shout of laughter as he leaned back against the wall. '*You* with an inferiority complex and basic insecurity! That's the best you've come up with so far. Who spun you that load of codswallop?'

'I read it in a book.' Lallie kept her smile going with difficulty. 'An American thing—*Know Your Hang-ups and How to Overcome Them*. It's been of tremendous help to me. I used to cower in corners like a mouse.'

'I don't believe it.' He put an arm about her shoulders and drew her into the sitting room where the fire which Nerys had lit earlier was burning brightly. 'When you're in a corner, little one, you don't cower, you never did. You come out spitting and with every claw ready to scratch. I see you've swallowed your pride enough to wear my woollies.'

Lallie fluttered her eyelashes as though she was in an agony of embarrassment. 'You said they wouldn't fit your lady friends, and they do help to cover my flat chest!'

'Another bit of basic insecurity?' The arm about her shoulders tightened and turned her to face him. 'It's not flat and you know it, so stop flirting with me or you'll get more than you bargain for.' His free hand seized her left one and raised the ruby ring to where she could see it. 'I've the right now and I'll have you down on that couch and carry out my own inspection. Taste and try before you buy, that's my motto. Even if the goods are a bit shopsoiled.'

'Back to square one,' she sighed, then stiffened as she heard the door open. It couldn't be Jonty, he'd have made much more noise, it must be Stella, and she softened herself, liftng her face to Owen's. 'Please,' she whispered, offering her mouth. She was close enough to see the little yellow flames and for a

second—but only a second—she regretted her behaviour. Then his mouth was on hers and regret
became a thing of the past. It was all right, she
thought while she was capable of thought, this playing with fire, and she wished she hadn't done it, but
there had been a devil driving her. Owen's mouth
was as hungry as her own, there was a warmth here,
a need, and she drew herself closer to it.

Something inside her was screaming, 'Out of your
depth', and reluctantly she drew back, unplastering
herself from him. He'd pounce on any sign of weakness, so she manufactured a bright smile that held a
tinge of mockery; it was self-mockery, but he wasn't
to know that.

'Missing your conferences, my love?' she whispered. 'You'd better get yourself off on one and
quickly, then you won't have to maul me!' She
moved languidly to look at Stella. 'Sorry,' she said
blandly. 'Owen and I were just discussing the
spring-cleaning.'

CHAPTER FIVE

OWEN pushed his breakfast plate aside and began a search of his pockets for pipe and tobacco before beginning the important ritual of shredding, stuffing the bowl, tapping it all down firmly and then lighting it. It all took time and Lallie looked at him from under her lashes while she buttered her toast. Over the past week or so, she had managed to organise herself into a routine so that most of her household chores were over by dinner time. But Owen was dawdling this morning, wasting his time and her own.

'What did you think of her?' The pipe was now going satisfactorily and smoke wreathed about his head.

Lallie raised an eyebrow. 'You mean Vi Turnbull, Jonty's shepherdess?'

'Mmm.' He leaned back in his chair studying her, watching the expressions flitting across her mobile face. 'Take your time about it,' he advised, 'and we've got plenty of that this morning—time, I mean. I've only one herd of milkers to inspect on a farm just outside Trellwyd, but I'm not due there until ten.'

She took her time and thought, surprised at how little there was to think about. She could see Vi in her mind's eye quite clearly, a big woman, good-looking but not a beauty—a quantity of curly brown hair;

cool, quiet brown eyes; a cool, quiet smile, but apart from that, there was nothing except the nebulous impression that Vi was cautious. Cautious about meeting people and cautious about what she said. Lallie could even have imagined the faint hostility she had thought she had seen in those cool brown eyes. Vi Turnbull had made very little impact. Lallie thought some more and her words came out slowly as though she was choosing them with care.

'I don't know what to think, because she's not a bit as I expected. I thought, with you saying "agricultural student", that she'd be much younger, more "with-it", but she's not. She's as old as Jonty, maybe even a bit older, and he's thirty, Isn't that a bit old for a student? But I like her, at least I think I do.' She frowned and then brightened. 'But it's nothing to do with me or anybody except her and Jonty, is it? and she seems very good for him, he's matured and much more self-confident. I think she may be exerting a steadying influence on him, he certainly needs it, and she seems to be a good sidekick as well. He needs that.'

'What on earth do you mean?' Owen pushed his cup across for refilling.

'Ha!' she crowed with delight. 'The great Owen Tudor missed something! You mean you didn't notice? Owen, I'm ashamed of you!'

'If you don't tell me what you're on about, you devious little brat,' he threatened, 'I'll come round this table and give you a leathering!'

'You'll have to control that nasty temper of yours,' she reproved. 'At least while I'm holding the teapot. I've got a very good aim, a bullseye every time at this distance.' She saw his eyes beginning to glow and continued hastily, 'Jonty talked about sheep, but only in relation to dogs. Sheepdog pedigrees—sheepdog pups—sheepdog training—sheepdog trials—you'd think, to listen to him, that he was a sheepdog breeder instead of a sheep farmer. It's quite obvious who does the actual work while he gets his dogs ready for the trials.' She put her head on one side, pausing for a moment. 'Do you think they really are . . . ?'

'Living together? Oh, I should think so.' Owen's smile glimmered. 'They're both personable, no wooden legs, false teeth or glass eyes—they're living together in the same house, it's rather small and pretty remote—they're working together. If nothing else, propinquity would do the rest.'

'She's in love with him, I think, although she's so self-contained, it's difficult to say,' Lallie said thoughtfully as she buttered a second slice of toast and then spread marmalade lavishly. She had been running about, seeing to Dwynwen, and hadn't started her breakfast until Owen had nearly finished his. 'I'm not so sure about Jonty either. They didn't give much away, they talked quite a bit, but never about themselves. Not that they had much chance, your Stella saw to that.' And she bit into her toast with a snap of her white teeth.

'*Not* my Stella,' he shook his head at her. 'I've told you about that, she's an old friend, that's all. One who needs a helping hand over a rough patch.'

'Your 'old friend' doesn't give that impression,' Lallie sniffed in a derogatory way. 'If she'd sat any closer to you yesterday evening, she'd have been in your lap. She was cuddling up to you like a second cardigan. Old friend indeed!'

'Jealous?'

'Not in the least,' she said disdainfully. 'She made me mad, that's all. Hanging on until I had to offer her tea, and spoiling everything. I think Vi and Jonty might have talked more about personal things if she hadn't been here. I tried, while we were in the kitchen washing up, but it wasn't any good—your friend detached herself from you and came offering to wipe up.'

'You sound jealous.' He looked at her quizzically through a cloud of smoke.

'Not me,' Lallie denied it vigorously. 'And I'd rather leave the subject of your old friend, she sticks in my throat, so let's go back to Jonty's shepherdess.'

'A lady with a past, do you think?'

'N-no,' she shook her head, 'and don't ask me questions like that, I'm not an expert on people. Why are you asking anyway? I suppose you've got some wriggly little plan to interfere, and I wish you wouldn't. I know Jonty's your brother, but he's a big boy now and he's happy, so why try to spoil it for him? You'd be better occupied trying to talk Dwynwen round so that she accepts Vi as part of the scenery—and you could, if you put your mind to it.' Lallie's mind flicked back to yesterday and she giggled.

'Vi's what Dwynny would call a "deep one",' she giggled again. 'All those leading questions your Stella asked, being all wide-eyed and innocent about them—she should have taken up the Law instead of hotel work, she'd have made a first rate Q.C. And all she had going home was a description and how they, Vi and Jonty, treated each other, although I suppose it's enough to build a mountain out of a molehill and start another round of gossip.'

Owen ignored most of this and concentrated on what was, to him, a sore point. 'Stella's not "my" Stella!'

'Sorry,' Lallie poured herself another cup of tea. 'I forgot—you must forgive me my little failings. You're being altruistic in that direction, aren't you?'

'I'm being nothing in that direction.' His eyes started to glint. 'How could I, an engaged man and only a blink away from marriage.'

It was at this point that a thought occurred to her, an unpleasant one and one which she hadn't contemplated before. She tried to dismiss it, but it wouldn't go.

'And what are people saying about us?' she asked in a hesitant tone, and then, as her courage built up, 'Wouldn't this propinquity thing apply to us, or does it only operate for Jonty and Vi? Is the great Owen Tudor above suspicion? Damn you, Owen, you've started a whole new train of thought, and I don't much like what I'm thinking. We're living here, in the same house, we're both quite personable, we're not related in any way, and as a chaperon, Dwynny's about as much good as a piece of cold haddock. There's also the matter of your reputation and mine as well; if they remember it. Is everybody drawing the same conclusions about us?'

'You haven't been here that long.' Owen relit his pipe which had gone out while they walked. 'But, given time, say another couple of weeks, and I should think they will.' He sounded quite serene. 'Would it bother you? After all, the blame is partly yours as well, you know. That little act you put on yesterday, for Stella's benefit, I presume,' his voice went up a couple of octaves as he mimicked her in a high falsetto. 'We were just discussing the spring-cleaning. You did that deliberately, Lallie, to give the worst possible effect.'

'I get carried away,' she grinned, and then so-bered, retreating into her shell and refusing to let her distaste show. 'But it shouldn't worry you, your reputation's about as black as ink already, and I shall be back in London as soon as Dwynny's fit, so it won't affect me.'

'As you say, my pretty.' His lips folded in a hard, tight line. 'After all, who am I to contradict you? You're the expert, you've been there before, haven't you?' And he rose and slammed out of the kitchen.

Lallie waited until she heard the front door slam as well and then started on her morning chores. It was something she didn't want to think about, that time in London. It had been painful enough, and that had been among thousands of strangers, people who didn't know her, who couldn't have cared whether she lived or died. It would be much worse here, where she was known, but—she shrugged her shoulders. She'd been through it once, she could do it again if she had to, and in any case, as she had said, she wasn't a permanent fixture. It would all blow over and she wouldn't even hear about it. There was nothing to worry about.

This comforting thought kept her reasonably happy until eleven o'clock when Stella came into the kitchen for coffee. There was an air of suppressed excitement about her and Lallie was glad Nerys was comfortably established in with Dwynwen. Stella's look was enough, and any comforting thoughts Lallie might have had vanished immediately—blown away in a gust of despair and indecision. Stella looked like a cat that had discovered a bowl of rich cream and who had gobbled the lot. She was almost licking her lips.

'A very nice tea yesterday, Lallie.' Even her tone was sardonic and condescending. 'I was able to tell my sister all about Jonty's woman.'

'Jonty's woman?' Lallie eyed Stella glacially. 'I presume you mean Miss Turnbull, but I don't see how you could have so much to tell. Vi seems very discreet.'

'Mmm.' Stella looked even more pleased. 'But every little helps, don't you think? My sister doesn't get about very much and she's interested in people, she likes to know what's going on. Did I tell you, one of her hobbies is a great scrapbook—she's also interested in the theatre. She had a very good voice, you know, and she was in several productions when she was younger, nothing in London, of course, although she did a whole season in Cardiff once, that was before she was married and the children came. After that, she couldn't take an active part any longer, so she started her scrapbook. She says it keeps her up to date with what's happening in the theatre world.'

'How nice. I've always said everybody should have a hobby, and this is a whacking great scrapbook, I suppose.' Lallie felt a chill creeping over her.

She would have liked to run away, to hide in with Dwynwen and Nerys, but pride stopped her. 'And thousands of cuttings,' she continued, 'all pasted in, probably a complete record of every show or play put on since she retired. It must make her quite an authority.'

'As you say, a complete record. She was showing it to me last night, we both found it very interesting.'

'Get to the point.' Lallie feigned uninterest. 'I suppose you do have a point?'

'The newspaper clippings were interesting, as I said.' Stella was enjoying every long-drawn-out moment. 'Especially the ones about Marla Lake, a firm favourite of my sister's. She used to be in musicals, you know, before she married, that's when her husband persuaded her to go straight. The cuttings about her cover five whole pages all to themselves. Of course, I didn't realise, not straight away. I was used to thinking of you as one of the Tudors—and then I remembered, you said I could call you Miss Moncke if I liked. But the photographs of you were very good, weren't they? You're quite photogenic. And what was it they called you, a pert little typist who'd been having a grubby affair with a successful man.'

'So,' Lallie shrugged and raised her eyebrows, 'you've found a juicy little titbit for everybody to rake over again. I should have thought they'd not find it so spicy the second time around.'

'But you aren't thinking of Owen.' Stella looked reproachful.

'Thinking of Owen!' Lallie snorted. 'It was my reputation that was in tatters, not his. Owen can look

after himself, he's been carrying on a pretty successful double life ever since he was old enough to
misbehave himself, and he's always come up smell-
ing of roses. You don't have to worry about him, he's
practically bullet-proof by now.'

'But I do worry.' Stella's eyes glittered like pale
blue glass. 'He's coming up for re-appointment, and
what will be the effect if the Council decides against
him? You know what it's like in this part of the world,
they could easily choose somebody else. I heard one
of the Councillors has a relative who wants the job.'
She sighed. 'There's bound to be talk—people are
so narrow-minded—his brother living with that
woman—and now you, living here with Owen.
People are going to say . . .'

'They're going to say that what I did once, I could
do again,' Lallie interrupted. 'Is that what you
mean?'

'It's Owen's career at stake,' Stella reminded her
gently. 'And it could very well affect his private
practice as well.'

'My career was at stake once,' Lallie reminded her
hardily. 'It's one thing I learned, you can get over a
thing like that.'

'But you didn't have a social position to lose.'
Stella was getting angry. 'You and Owen—you can't
compare his job with yours. He has a great deal of
responsibility, he's in daily contact with people,
people who matter.'

'And Shire Hall might turn up its nose at the
smell?' Lallie snorted again. 'Let them—and now, if
you don't mind, I think we've wasted enough time
this morning and I'm sure you have some typing to

do,' and she swept the untouched coffee pot from the table and tipped the contents down the sink before starting on a bowl of potatoes. She heard the kitchen door close and dropped her hands in the icy water with a groan of despair. Owen had let himself in for a load of trouble, if Stella was to be believed.

Poor Owen, only trying to do his best for Dwynwen. Her lips twitched into a softer curve and then straightened out into a hard line. Serve him right! Thinking he knew better than anybody, bulldozing people around to serve his own purpose.

One thing she was grateful for, that Nerys had been in with Dwynwen. The girl might have the mental age of a ten-year-old, but she would have absorbed every word said and retailed it faithfully. The twiddly bits would have been put in, adding to the impact of the original, and it would all have been passed over the counter of the post office with each pension book, stamp and postal order.

Lallie was still cold and impersonal when Owen returned for dinner. She had crept back into the hard little shell she had built for herself after the debacle in London. Stella joined them at the table, sitting opposite Nerys, and Lallie hoped that the woman would have the sense not to say anything. She found herself quite unable to sit with them, making polite and meaningless conversation as she loaded Dwynwen's tray, added her own plate to it and went into the housekeeper's room.

'Come to have a picnic,' she announced as she arranged the tray over Dwynwen's knees and sat on the edge of the bed to eat her own meal.

Dwynwen gave a soft cackle of laughter. 'Falling out again, you and Owen?'

'Certainly not!' Lallie looked virtuous. 'You know how Owen and I have always been. Never a cross word that wasn't meant.'

'Jonty was here yesterday.' The old lady wasn't asking a question, she was stating a fact. 'No, that Nerys didn't tell me—heard him, I did. I've got good ears even at my age.' Lallie decided to brazen it out.

'And his shepherdess,' she said quietly. 'She's rather nice.'

'Can't be,' Dwynwen said definitely. 'Not doing what she's doing. They should be married—living like that—get the whole family a bad name.'

'I think Jonty wants to marry her, I believe Vi's the one who's holding back.' Lallie laid her fork down and looked serious. 'She's a nice person, Dwynny, not at all what you think, and she's a hard worker. What's more important, she seems to be making Jonty very happy. She's not a young girl, you know. I believe she may be a bit older than he is and I think she's just the sort of person he needs. If she comes again, will you let me bring her in to see you?'

'Hmm.' Dwynwen gave it some thought while she scraped up minced beef. 'We'll see.'

'You might be able to show her the error of her ways,' Lallie chuckled. 'Think of it, Dwynny, a person led back into the paths of righteousness, and all by your efforts. You might even be able to talk her into marrying him, then there might be a baby and you could go visiting, you'd like that.'

'Stop your soft talking, you won't get round me.' Dwynwen finished off the last of her mashed potatoes and sighed with satisfaction before becoming stern again. 'I shall do as the Lord directs me.'

'Then ask Him to direct you to let Jonty and Vi come to tea again and to let you have them come in to see you,' Lallie suggested as she picked up the tray. 'Try, Dwynny. I think you're hurting Jonty by refusing to see him, and he's always thought a lot of you, he loves you.'

Lallie had to wait until well after tea before she had a chance to speak to Owen. Stella seemed to have glued herself to the typist's chair in the office, working long after her normal time for departure so that she once more had to be offered tea, and then Owen escorted her down the garden path and they stood talking by the gate where Stella's Mini was parked. Lallie watched them from the kitchen window. She didn't want to, but it was compulsive viewing.

Stella stood there in the biting wind, hardly seeming to notice the cold, her face turned up to his and her hand possessively on his sleeve. It made Lallie feel sick, and that was something that needed analysing. She wasn't blind to Owen's faults, he was an egotistical bastard, conceited, dictatorial, a womaniser—anything in skirts from seventeen to seventy, and he automatically turned on the charm, he couldn't help it, and for him, it was fun, he enjoyed every moment of it, damn him!

Lallie herself had her weakness for him, despite the way he'd treated her; she even loved him a bit. Here she caught herself up—not a bit, she loved him like mad, but wild horses wouldn't have dragged that admission from her except to herself. She

daren't even let it be seen, because once he found
out, he'd exploit it and her for all he was worth and
then she'd stand no chance at all. She'd made a life
for herself and was reasonably happy in it, but he'd
never let her keep it. Quietly, she withdrew into her
shell.

When Owen came back into the kitchen, rubbing
his hands and holding them out to the blaze in the
firebox, she had managed to become very calm and
self-contained, it put a fine edge on her tongue.

'Stella has a sister in Trellwyd,' she remarked in a
chilly voice. 'Has she told you about her?' And at the
shake of his head, 'She, the sister, is a theatre fan
with a scrapbook going back to the year dot, she's
also a devotee of Miss Marla Lake. How's that for a
coincidence?' At this point her feelings got the better
of her and she slammed the last plate into the rack
with force enough to split it in two.

Owen swooped on her like some monstrous bird of
prey to tow her away from the sink and into the
sitting-room. 'There's been a batch of poison brew-
ing up in you since dinnertime.' He pushed her into a
corner of the couch. 'You'd better get it up before it
chokes you—and in simple sentences, please, without the usual innuendo.'

'You mean you prefer me to be blunt?'

'You couldn't be that if you tried,' he glared at her.
'You've too sharp an edge on your vicious little
tongue. What's all this about a scrapbook and Marla
Lake, and why has it upset you?'

'Men!' Lallie spat the word at him. 'They haven't
the sense they were born with! Your Stella's seen that
scrapbook, she could even remember that lovely bit

where I was a 'pert little typist'. From now on, there'll be a path beaten to the sister's door while everybody refreshes their memories of little Lallie's fall from grace.' Her spurt of anger died, to be replaced by worry. 'I'm not so much concerned for myself, I've been through it once and I can go through it again, but your Stella says you're coming up for re-appointment and the present state of things here might go against you. It would be entirely your own fault, of course, and you'd have nobody but yourself to blame. I didn't ask to be dragged up here by the scruff of my neck, that was all your doing.'

'So it was,' he agreed amiably, dropping to sit beside her on the couch. 'What's the worry, then?'

'Because I don't think you'll blame yourself.' She looked up at him, even sitting together, his head was so much higher than her own. 'You'll find some way to blame me for ruining your career, I know you will. I've thought about it all afternoon and there doesn't seem to be anything I can do, although I suppose I could beg a bed from Jonty and Vi, just come up here during the daytime.'

'Working on the supposition that I don't make love during the daylight hours?'

'Something like that.' The humour of it struck her and she grinned. 'A sop to the public—they aren't to know you'd do it any time you wanted, midnight or high noon.' She felt him laugh rather than heard him. 'What's that for?' she demanded.

'I was just thinking what a blessing it is that you're not on the appointments committee. I'd not stand a chance—but not to worry, the board doesn't meet until June, we've got two clear months, and anything can happen in that time.'

'Like what?' Lallie refused to be mollified.

'Like we'll start making a good impression, get out where we're known and flaunt that ring around. Where is it, by the way?'

'Upstairs on the dressing table,' and at his look of disgust, 'I can't wear it when I'm cooking. I did the first day and it took me hours to get the pastry out of the setting, it's all fiddly bits.'

'I suppose you mean you don't like it,' Owen growled at her. 'Lord, you're an expensive wench! I'll take you to Aber and you can choose something more to your taste.'

'No, thank you,' she said primly. 'I'm quite happy with that one, I can't wear it for most of the time and that suits me fine.'

'But it doesn't suit me—and there's another thing which I don't like, that's your attitude when we're together. You don't give the right impression. You're either biting my head off or you're giving me black looks. You're supposed to look all Moon, Spoon and June, not as if you want to scratch my eyes out. If you could manage an expression halfway between starry-eyed wonderment and unfulfilled passion, we'd probably have the populace believing in us via Stella and Nerys.'

'The populace?' she squeaked. 'I thought this was for Dwynny's benefit. Besides, I wouldn't know how to do it.'

'You must have learned something from your golden oldies.' Owen moved in on her, crowding her back into a corner and fastening a firm hand in her hair. 'But if you didn't, here's your first lesson,' and his mouth came down on hers.

Behind her closed eyelids, moons and stars whirled magnificently, and then she felt her eyes fill with tears. This wasn't fair—he had all the know-how and he was crowding her, forcing a response she didn't want to give. Her hands went up to his hair, she fully intended to pull out handfuls of it, but her stupid fingers refused to obey her brain. Restlessly, she stirred against him.

He raised his head and looked down at her. 'Do that again.'

'What?' she whispered through smarting lips.

'Wriggle.' He pulled her closer to him. 'Your trouble, my girl, is that you've been kissing the wrong men.'

Some time later he raised his head from where his mouth had been caressing the hollow between her breasts. 'Do you want to go any further?' he murmured in a thick whisper, but before Lallie could either nod weakly or shake her head violently, the telephone rang from the hall.

Owen let it ring several times and then, when it seemed to threaten to go on ringing all evening if it wasn't answered, he slid to his feet with a stifled epithet which made her gasp at its vehemence. 'Stay where you are,' he paused briefly at the door. 'I'll be back.' But he wasn't.

Lallie heard his voice through the open door. 'Yes, love, I'll be there as soon as I can,' and he was gone, flinging out of the front door into the chill evening air.

She gave herself a few minutes to recover from the

assault on her senses before she tried to get to her feet. Even then, her legs felt too weak to support her and she was filled with a sense of deprivation as she slumped down on the rug by the fire. But she wasn't crying because she'd been deserted, not really, and her hands clenched into fists. She was weeping for her own stupid weakness, her own moronic idiocy, that she'd made herself so easy! But then she hadn't stood very much of a chance, not against Owen; he was a master at his own game.

Anger with him and with herself came spilling back, heating the little chill that had settled inside her when he went off to the phone and making her rage about his lazy 'I'll be back'. He was so sure of himself and of her. And then she started thinking about the phone call—Stella, she supposed, probably wanting to give him a fresh look at that damn scrapbook, and after he'd read it all over again, he'd go back to her cottage with her and soothe whatever little worry she had invented to get him down to Trellwyd. She shook her head and brushed the tears from her face with the back of her hand.

Once a fool, always a fool! Lallie rose to her feet and stuck her small chin out. Not Lallie, she vowed it by everything she held dear, then she scrambled to her feet, smoothed down her rumpled clothing and went off to the kitchen where there was plenty to do. Lay out the supper, make Dwynwen a drink, put things ready for the morning, and then she would go to bed so that when he came in, she would be fast asleep and there would be no repeat of her wild behaviour.

CHAPTER SIX

Dwynwen wasn't much help either. The old lady sat there in her bed, cuddling the warm mug and taking occasional sips while she looked very pleased with herself.

'You've been tottering to the bathroom,' Lallie accused. 'You know you're not supposed to, you wicked old lady! Wait till they bring you the walking aid next week, you're not safe with a stick.'

Dwynwen was unrepentant. 'Can't stand those bedpans, and I've been thinking about it. Better if you and Owen don't wait until I'm up and about. People'll be looking sideways at you, specially if you have the first baby pretty quick. There's no telling with the first, that's a fact. Could be a fortnight either way—they'll be counting up on their fingers. Can't have that, can we?'

Lallie felt a hot flush spread over her face, it felt as though it was travelling all over her, that there was no part of her which wasn't a fiery red. Dwynwen picked up the embarrassment as though she was a mind-reader.

'Been at it already, has he? Then you'd better not wait any longer.'

Lallie's flush deepened. She was always thrown by the way Dwynwen could change from an attitude of puritanical righteousness to one of down-to-earthiness without turning a hair or blinking an eyelid. She tried a jokey retort and hoped it wouldn't fall flat and that she wouldn't burst into tears.

'Dwynny!' she reproved with a tight smile. 'You've got improper thoughts on your mind, you've been dwelling on Jonty and Vi too much. You mustn't think we're all alike.'

Dwynwen drained the last drops from her mug and handed it over. 'Never met any that wasn't the same,' she snorted, 'and Owen's got a way with him, always had. Speak to him tomorrow, I will—better that way. One should avoid even the appearance of evil.'

'Don't you say a word!' Lallie was close to tears, she had been striving for control ever since Owen had been called away and she thought she was near breaking point. 'I've still got to think about it,' she made her voice as persuasive as possible. 'I don't know I'm all that keen on getting married straight away, it's a big step—I wouldn't like to make a mistake. I don't even know if we'd get on together. It's for life, isn't it, and I want to be sure.' She stood up from where she'd been sitting on the edge of the bed to make for the door, followed by Dwynwen's jeering cackle.

'There's lies for you!'

'Oh!' Lallie blushed once more. 'Go to sleep, you aggravating woman, and stop making things worse. 'If I want to marry Owen, and I'm not at all sure that I do, not at the present moment—he's not been exactly the lover boy recently—I wouldn't need your help!'

'Better a pinch of help when it's needed than a ton of pity when it's too late! Not made up your mind, ha!

Think I'm a fool, Lallie?' And Dwynwen slid down in bed and closed her eyes firmly. 'Put out the light as you go.'

Lallie went back to the kitchen where she made herself a hot drink and drank it slowly. Everything was building up on her and she didn't know which way to turn. The trouble was, she was in a sticky situation, one she couldn't get out of.

Nothing, but nothing would have made her abandon Dwynwen to the tender mercies of Stella Prentice, so she had to stay until the old housekeeper was on her feet again. Equally, the situation between herself and Owen was getting out of hand—it had grown to a state where she couldn't stay, so what to do?

Had she been mad all these years? Not to have known what was the matter with her? It hadn't been Owen she had been fighting, it had been herself, purely a defence mechanism and purely in the interests of self-protection. She'd loved him all the time. At this point, her mind crystallised into a firm determination, she would go on protecting herself, otherwise Owen would step in and take over, and how he would crow!

She'd seen too many other girls turn themselves into doormats beneath his lordly feet; he took their adulation and he pitied them as he would pity her, only with her, it would be worse. She discounted his flirtations, the local ones anyway, they were only passing things, they didn't mean much, but his weekend 'conferences'—she shrugged; they didn't mean much either.

She found herself feeling sorry for Stella, although

she knew that as soon as she saw her again, her pity would be swamped in a wave of dislike. In fact, Lallie didn't need to see her again to start disliking. Stella had asked for all she got, she should have known better than to take Owen seriously, and, following from this, Lallie herself knew better than to take him seriously. He was the perennial bachelor gay and he'd probably stay that way until the day he died— he'd be quite likely to wink at a female mourner from his coffin if the female was young and nubile!

Weary with too much fruitless thought, she went back to the sitting room and chose a couple of books to take upstairs to bed. She had a hot bath, scrambled into bed, read a few pages, switched off the light and counted sheep. She did everything she knew to induce sleep, but it wouldn't come. She found herself listening for the sound of the Land Rover coming up the hill to the farmyard, listening for the slam of the door, and finally, at half past two, she gave up all thoughts of sleep. Her mouth was dry, her eyes were hot and smarting and she slid out of bed, struggled into a robe and went down to the kitchen where she made herself a cup of tea.

At three o'clock, she heard him come in and stood up to tie her robe more firmly about herself before going to switch on the kettle and empty away the teapot. He came down the passage with a dragging step as though he was very tired, and when he entered the kitchen, Lallie was busying herself making fresh tea.

'I thought you'd be late,' she said without turning from the counter. 'Did you have a nice time?'

'No, I haven't had a nice time!' and the concen-

trated venom in his voice made her whirl to face him.
He had flung himself into a chair and there was a
greyness under the tan of his face.

'Wasn't she nice to you?' Lallie asked with a
smirk.

'No, she wasn't. If you must know, she stood on
my foot.'

'Ha!' she chuckled, 'and now it's you who has the
"little sprain". Serve you right—but don't worry,
you'll be able to get about on it tomorrow—that's
what you told me, isn't it?' She brought a steaming
cup of tea to the table and plonked it by his elbow. 'A
bit of strapping, a couple of aspirin . . .'

He seized her wrist. 'Do you know how much she
weighed?'

Lallie treated the question lightly.

'About eight and a half stone,' she giggled. 'That's
only a rough estimate, though, but it can't be much
more. Stella's fairly tall, but she's very slim. Serve
you right, anyway.'

'Stella?' Owen's voice rose in indignation. 'What's
Stella got to do with it? I'm talking about a cow! How
would you like half a ton of pregnant moo-moo
treading all over your toes—and to add insult to
injury, she dropped her calf on me. Get me some
aspirin and the whisky bottle.'

Lallie stifled relieved laughter, happiness swim-
ming up in her until she thought she would explode
with the relief. She'd been so convinced he'd gone to
see Stella, she hadn't even considered it might have
been a working call. 'I thought you'd been with
a woman,' she explained between giggles of near
hysteria.

'The only woman I've seen tonight,' his voice was dangerously calm, 'was a fifty-year-old Sister at the hospital. She had a face like a hatchet and a sadistic disposition, nearly as bad as yours. She also had the biggest syringeful of antibiotics I've ever seen in my life, and she took a great deal of pleasure in sticking it in my backside.'

'Poor Owen!' Lallie became solemn. 'Is it a bad sprain?'

'Two toes broken—and don't you dare say it serves me right! The damn beast tramped all over me and her hooves cut my wellies to pieces.' He bent over and removed with difficulty a shredded gumboot, inspected his foot and held it out for her to see. 'Cut my foot as well, that's why the antibiotics. Where's the whisky?'

'I don't think you should,' she demurred. 'It might quarrel with the injection. Have another cup of tea and some aspirin.' She sat down on her knees to inspect the damage, gingerly taking off his sock to disclose some stained bandaging. 'If it's a break, shouldn't it be in plaster?'

'Toes don't get plastered, not the small ones— they'll heal themselves.' He winced as she gently probed among the wrappings. 'Lord! I could do with a drink.'

'You're not getting one.' Lallie scrambled to her feet, hitching her robe about her and pushing her plait of hair back over her shoulder. 'It'll inflame your blood or something.'

'Bloody women,' he growled. 'They think they know everything. If I can't have a drink, I'm going to bed, and you can phone the County Office in the morning, tell 'em I won't be available—then you'd better phone old Meredith in Trellwyd and tell him to take any calls for me.'

'That's right,' Lallie smiled. 'You go up, get yourself cleaned up a bit—you look as though you've bedded down with that cow—and I'll bring you up the aspirin and another cup of tea.' She walked behind him to the bottom of the stairs and watched as he hobbled up, then when he was halfway, she called softly, 'You'd better have a shower or a bath—no, not a bath, you'll get the dressing wet—have a shower and try to keep your foot out of it. You smell something 'orrible! Did she really drop the calf on you?'

He turned to look down on her. 'Right in my lap when I was on my knees, groaning in agony, and then she looked at me with eyes full of mother love and licked my face!'

'Ten minutes,' Lallie giggled. 'I'll drop a clean change on the bathroom stool for you, so don't be modest and lock the door.'

When she brought up the tea later, he was lying in bed, his face still rather grey and the lines from his nose to his mouth were etched more deeply with pain.

'You won't give me a drink?' and when she shook her head, 'Then stay with me for a while, it's hurting like hell!'

'Stay with you? Owen, are you mad?' Indignation pushed her voice up to a squeak as she turned from him to adjust the lampshade so that it didn't throw the light in his face.

'Don't be a bigger fool than you are normally,

Lallie,' he hissed at her. 'I'm in no condition, and I'm not in the mood for bedtime romps. I wouldn't even make a pass at Raquel Welch if she was lying naked beside me. There's not much of the night left, but it's going to seem like eternity.'

'Very well.' Lallie put the cup on the bedside table and sat down on the edge of the bed. She couldn't recall Owen ever being ill in all the years she'd known him. There had never been anything wrong with him before and Dwynwen always said that men were dreadful patients. 'Just for a while, until you go to sleep.'

Quietly, she began to talk, little anecdotes from long ago—'do you remembers'—her plans for a Greek holiday this year and the stratagems she'd used to save up for it, until her words were lost in a mammoth yawn and the sleep which she hadn't been able to find at half past ten swept over her and her eyes closed. She didn't feel herself toppling pillow-wards as she slid into a warm darkness which was more comfortable than anything she'd ever known. She gave a sleepy little grunt of satisfaction and stopped registering anything.

A bar of bright sunlight across her closed eyelids woke her and she let her eyes wander over those parts of the room she could see, frowning meanwhile at the unfamiliar surroundings. The door and window weren't where they should be and the wallpaper was strange. Then memory returned in a rush and she groaned as her eyes met Owen's. She opened her mouth to speak, but he put a hand over it.

'Don't make a row. It's eight o'clock and Nerys has just arrived. I heard her a few minutes ago.'

Silently, Lallie slid out of the bed, untangling the folds of her robe from where they were wound round her legs. 'Why didn't you wake me earlier?' she muttered.

'You're not blushing,' he accused.

It steadied her, effectively killing any embarrassment. 'With *my* reputation?' she said scornfully. 'Proof positive for you because I'm not as red as a turkeycock?—I'm white with fear, if you're really interested. How long have you been awake? And why didn't you wake me earlier instead of leaving it till the last minute? Oh God, Owen, I hate you! Stop grinning or I'll break the toes on your other foot!' And she was at the door, peering cautiously along the passage. 'And why,' she demanded, turning back to him, a scolding note in her voice, 'why, when I put you out a clean change of things, can't you wear them?'

'Never did, never do,' he answered, but she was far too busy making sure there was nobody about before she fled back to her own room, where she grabbed herself a handful of clean underwear and steadied her pace to a dignified walk as she crossed to the bathroom.

When she emerged, it was to find Nerys wandering about the passage like a lost soul and bearing a rapidly cooling cup of tea.

'You were late down this morning,' the girl looked her usual vacuous self, 'and I've just looked in on Owen, but he's still asleep. Shall I wake him? I could give him this cup of tea.'

'Not this morning.' Lallie belted her robe more firmly over her bra and panties. 'He had a bit of an accident last night, a cow stood on him and hurt his foot— he didn't come in till three. We'd better let him sleep. Here, give it to me,' and she seized the wavery teacup and drank the contents thirstily. 'I'll dress and be down straight away.'

Before she went into the kitchen, she spent a few minutes on the phone, ringing Mr Meredith in Trellwyd—it wasn't any good ringing the County Offices yet, they didn't start work until nine, so she could safely leave that to Stella. It was one job at which she excelled, making calls and answering the phone— about the only one. Lallie grimaced; as a typist, Stella was hopeless.

The telephone call concluded, she watched Nerys' latest efforts, which entailed negotiating the staircase with soiled clothing piled so high in her arms she couldn't see over the top.

'Washing again today?' she queried—Dwynwen had only ever washed on Mondays. 'Isn't it a bother doing it frequently? You have to light that copper, the dreadful old thing.'

Nerys gave her a sly grin. 'Not since Dwynwen,' she hastily corrected herself, 'Miss Roberts has been ill. Owen put in a lovely electric washing machine and a tumble dryer when they brought the electricity up from the farm, but she—Miss Roberts—wouldn't let me use it, she said it was too dangerous and it didn't get things clean, but I'm using it now. Lovely in the winter, it'll be.'

They both turned to look as Stella let herself in through the front door, ignoring them as she made her way to the office.

'Face in a knot this morning!' Nerys' whisper

reached Lallie as the girl made her way to the kitchen. 'Proper put out, isn't she?'

Lallie followed behind picking up the odd towel and handkerchief which dropped off the pile on the way. She opened the door so that the girl could get out to the washhouse and then came back to start breakfast.

'Has Owen left already?' Stella had come in silently, she was wearing flat shoes this morning, Guccitype things, and her legs looked beautiful in them. They'd look beautiful in anything, Lallie decided savagely, they were that type of legs.

'He's still in bed,' she answered shortly. 'He had an accident last night, so he's taken the day off to get over it. That reminds me, will you ring the County Offices and tell them he's not available today. Did you want him?'

'Yes.' Stella's reply was languid but there was a fretful twist to her mouth. 'Actually, I expected him to call in on me last night, I waited quite a while.'

'I expect the accident drove it out of his mind.' Lallie filled the kettle and switched it on before beginning on Dwynwen's breakfast. She wasn't eager to help, but she didn't want to be thought hardhearted. 'Is there anything I can do?'

'I hardly think so,' Stella brushed aside the offer of help as though the matter was too important to be discussed with the kitchen staff. 'I'll wait till he comes down,' and Lallie, who had been going to offer a cup of tea, a piece of toast and some sympathy, if Stella needed it, clammed up.

'Suit yourself,' she said shortly. 'I'm taking him up

this cup of tea, and if he's awake, I'll tell him you want to speak to him.'

'Do that.' Stella was sharply definite as she went back to the office.

Lallie didn't hurry, the brush-off had upset her equilibrium which had already suffered a nasty jolt this morning. She made Dwynwen's scrambled egg and soft toast, added a cup of tea to the tray and when she took it in, she took her time about retailing the news of Owen's accident.

'Two small toes broken and some lacerations,' she concluded. 'He was in a filthy temper, especially when I wouldn't give him the whisky bottle.' Of the rest she said nothing, she didn't want to upset Dwynwen's strict chapel conscience which might be rampant this morning. She tapped at Owen's door and swished in to find him sitting, dressed only in a pair of cord slacks and one sock, on the side of the bed and winding a fresh dressing about his foot. There seemed to be a lot of bruising and she frowned at it, but when she raised her eyes to his, his look was sardonic.

'Sleep well?' he enquired.

'Wonderfully.' She glared at him and then changed her expression for one of sweet reminiscence. 'I always do when I have somebody to cuddle up to.'

'And you cuddle so nicely.' Owen finished winding the bandage, pinned it and looked up into her face. 'I'd have done something about it if this foot hadn't been hurting so much.'

'Well, at least you're honest,' she grimned wolfishly at him. 'Admitting it was only pain that stopped you. Lots of men would have claimed to be too honourable.' She changed the subject swiftly. 'Stella's fretting for you. She's downstairs, champing at the bit—you didn't call on her last night and she has some private business she wants to discuss with you. You'd better come down and soothe her before she loses that monumental calm.'

'It was a question of priorities, you bitter little weed,' Owen grinned back in an equally wolfish fashion. 'Another lady had first call on my attentions last night, a Welsh Black called Glenys. Sorry I had to skip out on you, but she was in difficulties, the calf was the wrong way round—we worked hard on her and she repaid me by treading all over me. That's gratitude for you!'

'Something which a female should have done to you years ago,' she shot back at him. 'It might have deflated that massive ego of yours!' She gestured at the tea on the bedside table. 'Drink that and hurry on down, your Stella's waiting and I haven't had my breakfast yet.'

'A nice little calf,' he murmured, 'and in remembrance of what her coming into the world had interrupted, I persuaded them to call her Lallie.' She let him have the last word as a sop to his ego, merely sniffing as she slammed the door behind her.

It was eleven o'clock before Lallie heard the cause of Stella's bad temper, and then, as far as she was concerned, it was a blessing in disguise.

'I've already told Owen,' Stella said plaintively. 'The hotel where I'm to be manageress was scheduled to open for Easter and working on that assumption, I'd let my cottage to summer visitors as from that date and I've got bookings for it right through to September. Now the hotel opening has been delayed, the alterations won't be finished in time and I don't think we'll manage an opening before the Spring Bank Holiday. I asked Owen,' here she turned to gaze at him sweetly over the rim of her coffee cup, 'I asked him if he knew of a room in Aber or even hereabouts, I want to vacate my cottage in a week's time at the latest so that my sister can decorate and have everything clean and fresh for the summer visitors.' She smiled smugly. 'Owen says he's sure you'll be able to fit me in here, any little corner would do as long as there's plenty of wardrobe space. I do so hate having to crush my clothes.'

'It's all right with you, Lallie?' That was Owen deferring to her, it was a nice gesture, but it meant nothing, he didn't care whether it was all right with her or not, but she didn't care. The problem of finding an odd corner with the large hanging space for clothes was one which she shelved for the time being; there were other things which were more important. She was getting a fare-paying chaperon and one with an eagle eye—which would stop Owen's little gallop, so she beamed all over her face. She had her own axe to grind!

'It's a splendid idea,' she enthused. 'Stella will be on hand to answer that damn phone, it's driving me mad, but there are a few points, I meant to bring them up at a suitable moment, and this seems most suitable to me.' She looked up at Owen with a melting glance. 'This place is so old-fashioned, darling,' she laid particular emphasis on the 'darling'. 'I'd like a few alterations.'

'Sounds ominous.' He surveyed her lazily. 'When you start asking for things in that tone, as though butter wouldn't melt in your mouth, I get the feeling that everything's going to be turned upside down.'

'You always did have the worst opinion of me,' she murmured softly while her eyes glittered. 'I want an electric cooker, Owen. You can throw out that bottled gas thing in the scullery, Dwynwen won't eat anything cooked on or in it—and I'd like a dishwasher as well.'

'Is that all?'

'Not quite.' She dropped all signs of wheedling and became cool and business like. 'Come Spring and summer, this kitchen gets too hot with this solid fuel cooker, but we have to keep it going because of the hot water, so I'd like an immersion heater, an electric one. And then, when Stella does go to her hotel, I suppose you've elected me to do the typing?'

'Who else, my love?' Owen's eyes were now shining with the light of battle. It was catching, and her own eyes glowed with relish.

'Then I want an electric typewriter, a standard office model, nothing fancy but with a carriage big enough for tabulating. You can throw that old thing out,' she nodded in the direction of the office where an ancient Imperial stood on the smaller of the two desks. 'Either that or you can donate it to a museum where they can put it on show, labelled "ancient artefact". And you can install a telephone answering machine as well.'

'And I was going to replace the Land Rover,' he mourned.

'You can do that any time,' she murmured. 'Out of the petty cash!'

'You drive a hard bargain.'

'Mmm,' she nodded complacently. 'But look who I had to teach me!'

CHAPTER SEVEN

STELLA delayed over her coffee for as long as possible, but eventually she had to go to answer the telephone and Owen stretched himself in his chair with a perceptible wince as his foot touched the table leg.

'You're looking like a cat fed on cream, Lallie,' his eyes glinted. 'What's pleased you so much? You're not that fond of Stella.'

'Not fond at all,' she agreed, 'but you've just provided me with a ready-made chaperon. There can't be any gossip now.'

'They could say I've taken advantage of Dwynwen's illness to start my own private harem,' he pointed out, an amused smile touching his lips, and she wagged her head at him reprovingly.

'That's what they might say in the Rugby Club, the men there have very coarse minds, but it's not what the women will say, and it's the women who do the gossiping. It's what they say that counts, not what a lot of overgrown schoolboys whisper over their beer mugs.'

'And where are you going to sleep Stella? What little corner do you have in mind for her?'

Lallie considered, her head on one side and her lips pursed in thought. The conclusion at which she arrived was one which didn't please her—it wasn't a particularly happy one, but beggars can't be choosers—it was the only one possible.

'I *could* put her in your room,' she shook her head, 'but there isn't enough wardrobe space, so I'm afraid she'll have to have mine, it's the only one with a decent sized wardrobe.'

'And where will you go?'

'I think,' her eyes sparkled aggravatingly, 'I think I'll sleep in yours.'

'Glad to have you any time,' Owen chuckled, 'and it won't be a novel experience for you, will it?'

'If that's the way you're going to take it,' she spat the words at him, making no attempt to hide her temper, 'I shall go straight down to Jonty's and you and Stella can sleep wherever you fancy—and,' she paused to give the words more effect. 'I bet I know where your Stella fancies!'

'You coarse little bitch!' His hand shot out and fastened on her wrist. 'You bloody little termagant! If I hear one more remark like that from you, I'll scrub your mouth out with soap!'

Lallie maintained her dignity with difficulty, her wrist felt as though it was being mangled. Her face whitened with the pain of it and she spoke through stiff lips and in an icy voice.

'How unoriginal can you get? That's the second time you've threatened me with that, and that does it! Maybe I did let my temper run away with me and maybe it wasn't a very nice thing to say. I apologise for it, of course, but I'm not staying here to be threatened!' She made to rise, but his fingers clamped on her wrist and he increased the pressure slightly so that she caught her breath on a sob. 'I'm going to Jonty's,' she repeated wildly, 'and you can't stop me!'

'Can't I?' He raised his eyebrows at her. 'And keep your voice down, or do you want everybody to know we're quarrelling?'

'Anybody can know for all I care!' Lallie struggled to free herself, scratching at his enfolding fingers. 'Let me go, you pig—time might have given you a few grey hairs, but it hasn't improved you one little bit! You're just the same as you always were, a dictator, and I'm not putting up with it a moment longer!'

'You're not going anywhere,' even his smile was a threat, 'and you're certainly not going running to Jonty. He's got something good going for him and I'm not letting you spoil it.'

'Spoil it?' She gasped with outrage. 'When have I ever . . .'

'. . .All the time,' he interrupted. 'Ever since you were about sixteen. You always ran to him, you had him so he didn't know whether he was coming or going. The poor young fool thought the sun shone out of your eyes. Well, he's over it now and you're not starting that up all over again.'

'I don't believe you,' she said truculently, while she remembered. She always had run to Jonty and he'd always been kind to her. Every time she'd had one of her monumental rows with Owen, Jonty had always been waiting in the wings to give her comfort—to build up her morale which Owen was so good at shattering. He'd pet her and make her feel better again. 'It wasn't like that,' she muttered. 'Jonty was my friend.'

'There wasn't much "friendship" about it, at least not as far as Jonty was concerned, he had it badly and he was still wet behind the ears, poor kid. Maybe that was all it was to you, but you never could see farther than the end of your nose, and every thought was about Lallie, you never noticed the effect you had on anyone else. It wasn't like that for my kid brother, Lallie, he wanted to marry you—you had him tied up in knots. All right,' as she started to protest, 'I'll give you the benefit of the doubt, maybe you didn't realise what you were doing to him, but you nearly broke up this family, what there was left of it. He wouldn't understand when I disapproved of his marrying you. So you had to go.'

'I had to go?' She looked at him with puzzlement.

'It was either that or having him try to talk you into running away with him, and I couldn't chance that, you might have agreed just to spite me.' She looked at Owen's face and saw the pain in his eyes. 'He wasn't up to your weight, girl—you'd have made a doormat out of him. There'd never been an idea in his head you hadn't put there, La Belle Dame sans Merci had nothing on you!'

'Ha!' she was still defiant. 'But I went, Owen, and it had nothing to do with you, did it? I went under my own steam just as soon as I could and,' at this point, she became triumphant. 'You didn't send me away either, if I remember rightly, you told me I wasn't to go.'

The pressure on her wrist relaxed and she sat nursing her bruised bones, her mouth in a gleeful curve, although she felt more like crying.

'Exactly!' Owen almost sneered at her stupidity. 'I told you not to go, didn't I? I told you you had to stay on another year in school, get that other "A" level. Lord, Lallie, after knowing you since you were four years old, do you think I didn't know how to manage you?'

'I wasn't that bad,' she protested sullenly.

'You were worse!' he ripped back at her. 'Dwynwen, Jonty, Dorcas, even my father, they all spoiled you rotten. The only person in the house you ever paid any attention to was your mother.'

'And you were always jealous of her,' she glared at him.

'Don't be stupid. Do you think I've been nursing a "wicked stepmother" complex all these years? Your mother was a lovely little lady, she made my father very happy for the few years they had together, and I was very fond of her. Jealous of her? You couldn't be more wrong. The only thing I could never understand was how she managed to produce such a shocking little daughter.'

'Same here but different.' Lallie regained some of her poise. 'I liked your father very much, he was a wonderful man and Mummy was very happy with him too. So it just goes to show that this heredity thing doesn't work, or perhaps you're not the real Owen after all. Maybe you were left out on the hills on Midsummer Eve and the fairies stole you away, because what they left in your place was one of the Lordly Ones. You're cruel, Owen.'

'And I'll be a damn sight crueller if you start up your tricks with Jonty again,' he riposted. 'I want your promise and I'll accept it—you don't usually break them—You won't go messing things up for Jonty and Vi!'

'I thought you didn't approve . . .'

'Of course I approve,' he broke in on her. 'I only asked what you thought about her to make sure you had no designs in that direction. One word out of you and I'd have . . .'

'. . . And what would you have done?' Lallie managed a weak giggle.

'Put Plan B into operation.' He rose and limped round the table to stand over her. 'Now, shall we start all over again, cut out the rough stuff and be sensible. There's no need for us to be quarrelling all the time. Try me, Lallie, you'll find I'm quite easy to get on with.'

'As long as you're getting your own way.' She wasn't beaten and she wasn't going to give too much away.

'That too,' he smiled at her, and she caught her breath on a half sob. Like this, he was damn well irresistible and she could feel herself weakening. He was using her as he used anybody he needed when he needed them, and it wasn't fair. He turned on the charm and she nearly grovelled—nearly but not quite. 'Pax?' he enquired softly.

'Pax,' she agreed but with her fingers crossed.

'Then we'll have some fresh coffee and you can get me another couple of aspirin to take with it.' Owen paused reflectively. 'And don't bother your head about sleeping arrangements, you can have my room, if that's what you want. I'll move across to the old part of the house, sleep where my father used to. Dwynwen did it out last year after we had the roof repaired. You could go there yourself, but it's a long way from the kitchen, it'll be more convenient for you to have mine.'

'So much consideration!' Lallie couldn't help herself and the words came out with bitter force.

'Ah!' he warned. 'Don't start again. We agreed to bury the hatchet, didn't we?'

'It's what I've always wanted,' she murmured, the aggravating sparkle once more lighting her eyes. 'To bury it, I mean—preferably in you! Whoops!' she covered her mouth with her fingers for a second and then removed them to disclose a wide, remorseful grin. 'I shouldn't have said that, should I? You'll have to forgive me a momentary lapse. I can't help it, it's a habit I've got into.'

'I know.' He looked as rueful as she. 'Let's hate Owen! Curb it, Lallie, just make your brain work a little less swiftly. You always were pretty devastating at repartee.'

'It takes the place of brawn and muscle,' she nodded wisely. 'I haven't got either of those, I had to develop something in their stead, I couldn't go about without any defence, could I?'

'No,' he chuckled, 'but you used to smile a lot more than you do now, and if I remember rightly, you weren't quite as cutting. And what's happened to your laughter?'

'Beaten out of me,' she admitted mournfully. 'All your fault, of course.' She poured out the fresh coffee and went across to the dresser for the bottle of aspirin.

'Mmm,' his eyes twinkled as she gravely put two tablets by his cup and saucer, 'I'll admit that or part of it. A long time ago, I had a decision to make, and I think—no, that's not right—I *know* now I made the wrong one. How's that for an apology?'

'A bit loose, if you know what I mean, but I'll accept it knowing I won't get a better.' She gestured at his cup. 'Drink that and take your pills. How's the foot this morning?'

'Bloody awful.' Owen treated her to his famous smile. 'But we start afresh, is that agreed?'

'Tentatively.' She shrank back within herself, refusing to give very much ground. That smile had gone straight to her heart and if she wasn't very careful, he'd walk all over her. 'We'll see how we go on. When will Stella be coming?'

'Next week. Think you can cope?'

'Oh, I can cope with anything.' Her face took on a sadness and her eyes grew bleak. 'London taught me that—a lesson well learned, if I do say so myself as shouldn't!'

Lallie walked slowly back up the valley, a black and white collie trailing at her heels. It wasn't a nice day, the March winds had blown themselves out and April had come in, dull and misty. There had been several nice spells, though, days when she'd spent afternoons weeding or planting out lettuce in the sheltered kitchen garden at the back of the house, but now April was nearly gone. Time hadn't flown, but it had passed, which was a good thing.

Dwynwen was improving steadily, she was going about with her walking aid, but never beyond the confines of her own flat—and that was because of Stella's presence in the house, Lallie was sure. Once or twice Lallie had tried to coax her into the kitchen, but Dwynwen had refused and Lallie was almost certain she hadn't imagined the lightning gleam of fear in the old lady's sharp black eyes.

'Come on, Dwynny,' she had wheedled once. 'Nobody's going to bite you. We could have a nice cup of tea and it would be a change of scene for you. You must be fed up with just these bedroom and sitting room walls. I should be after all this time.'

'What's the matter with them?' Dwynwen had demanded sharply. 'Nice, aren't they? Suits me, anyway, even if you don't like my roses.' Roses were Dwynwen's favourite and when it came to interior decoration, she went to town on them. They scrambled all over the wallpaper, they clustered round her own private crockery and they embellished the cream curtains in a riotous scramble from top to bottom.

Lallie had shrugged, reluctant to use any further persuasion, and had brought the tea-tray into Dwynwen's sitting room without demur. And yet, as a lodger, Stella wasn't too bad. She was neat, almost to the point of it being a fad, and except for a few times when she had tried to instil instincts of economy in Lallie's unreceptive mind, she didn't interfere too much.

'It would be so much simpler for you,' she had pointed out, 'if you'd think of daily expenses as far as running the house is concerned. Allow yourself so much money, so much food every day. Any decent book will tell you how much a person needs to eat, calories, proteins and things, and if you were to keep that in mind, you'd soon find yourself having less waste. So many slices of meat, so many sprouts per person . . .'

'And Jonty's pigs would go very hungry,' Lallie passed it off with a smile. 'We waste very little, Stella. What we don't eat ourselves,' she shrugged, 'there's always the dogs, and as I said, Jonty's pigs.'

It wasn't Stella's fault, she comforted herself. Stella had been in catering, she was going to manage a fair-sized hotel, and it probably offended her business sense to see extra cooked just in case anybody was especially hungry. What she would have objected to was the implication that she was lining her pockets out of the housekeeping, but Stella was careful, she never implied such a thing, not out loud.

Lallie counted the slow passing days, three weeks and a bit. Quiet because Owen had been busy, spending very little time at home, she sniffed at her own dullness; she missed the fights and she was fed up with keeping a guard on her tongue.

This afternoon she had taken her weekly walk over to Jonty's place, but as usual, he was busy with his dogs, training for the coming trials, and there was only Vi in the house. A Vi Lallie didn't seem ever to get any closer to. Dwynwen, spurred on by a letter from Dorcas, had been on and on about people getting married and Lallie had intended, if the occasion arose, to sound Vi out as to whether there was any possibility of wedding bells in the foreseeable future.

But the opportunity hadn't arisen. Vi was her usual guardedly friendly self, not the sort of person of whom one could ask such a thing straight out. They had eaten scones fresh from the oven and drunk strong tea before the kitchen fire, but it hadn't been a rewarding visit.

Vi had been perfectly willing to talk about her youth in Northumberland, but she had gently steered the conversation away from the present, and with no Jonty there, Lallie just didn't have the courage to bring up the subject. If he'd been present, she could have made a joke of it, but not with Vi.

Lallie pushed open the farmyard gate and then looked up towards Bryn Celyn, then she shook her head. She didn't want to go back, not yet, so she turned aside to push open the doors of the old barn. In the dimness, she skirted a tractor, Owen's Bentley and various pieces of farm equipment, and found herself a quiet corner where she dropped onto a pile of sacks, drawing her knees up to her chin.

'Home soon,' she comforted the dog, who lay down beside her and put a cold wet nose on her foot while she sank into dejection. After about ten minutes while her brain did mental athletics, trying to find a solution to being in two places at the same time, here with Dwynwen and away from Owen, she heard the Land Rover draw into the yard, there came the slam of the door after the engine had coughed and died and then no further sound until a shadow appeared in the square of light which was the barn door and Owen was walking towards her,

'Can't I get any peace anywhere?' Lallie demanded bitterly.

'Peace? What do you want peace for?' He dropped his long length beside her and stretched out on the sacks.

'I'm having a little brood on the injustice of life in

general and mine in particular, so go away, I brood better on my own.' She kept her chin on her knees and refused to look anywhere but at the barn door.

'Injustice!' Owen seemed to find the idea rather silly, because he snorted, choking back laughter. 'Don't be so dramatic, *anwylyd*. Just because you've had a quiet time these past few weeks, that's no reason for you to go into a decline and start talking about injustice as though everybody's been getting at you!'

Lallie still didn't look at him, she began talking, more as though she was speaking to herself and she didn't have an audience. 'I like a peaceful life, and I had one, in London. I had a good job, a nice little flat, although you turned up your nose at it, and I had no worries. There was nobody to bother me.'

'And who's bothering you now?' He didn't sound sympathetic.

She picked up a piece of straw and started to pull it between her fingers. 'I had enough money to live on, I could even save towards my holidays. I was going to Greece this year, did you know that? That old trouble had been forgotten, nobody kept harping on about it or saying 'Lallie, what a naughty girl you were'. And then you came and turned everything upside down.'

'Cry on my shoulder,' he offered cynically, 'and I'll shed a few tears for you—poor little Lallie, she can't stand the quiet life.'

'Wrong again,' this time she turned to look at him. 'I like a quiet life, it's just that I'm not getting it, and it's all your fault,' she added morosely.

'When wasn't it my fault?' Owen raised an eyebrow at her. 'Ever since you were about fourteen, you've been blaming me for anything that went wrong in your little world, and I'm fed up with it.'

'So!' she sniffed. 'You generally were to blame, but I'm not going to talk any more about it, not to you—you haven't a scrap of sympathy or understanding in your whole body.' And she dropped her chin back on to her knees and stared once more out of the doorway.

'I went over to see Jonty and Vi this afternoon,' she continued. 'I thought I might ask Vi why they didn't get married, but when I arrived there, when she invited me in, gave me scones and tea, I couldn't. The words just wouldn't come out.'

'Very wise of you, not asking.' He was unsympathetic about that as well. 'You'd only have landed yourself in trouble. Some people are more private than others, and I think Vi's one of them.'

Lallie resumed her straw pulling, this time with a longer piece. 'It would have helped, though,' she muttered. 'I might have been able to quiet Dwynny down a bit.'

'Oh lord! Has she started on that again?' Owen arranged himself more comfortably, rolling over until he was flat on his back. 'I thought she was beginning to accept . . .'

'Which just shows how much attention you pay to her!' Disturbed out of her lethargy, Lallie said it with a snap. 'You go in to see her a couple of times a day and yet you don't see what's in front of your eyes. Men!'

'And what should I see?' He sounded amused, as though he was humouring a small, sulky child.

'Fear!' She sat up straight. 'You've never known what that was, have you, Owen, but Dwynwen's full of it, and it's worse since you had Stella come to stay.'

'I had your permission,' he pointed out, 'and then it was only on your conditions. Do you know what the cooker and dishwasher cost me?'

'And I think she's just beginning to realise how inadequate I am,' Lallie continued as though he hadn't spoken. 'I mean my appearance is inadequate, so you can't blame her, not really. She takes a look at me, remembers what Stella looks like and she knows that nobody in their right mind would prefer me. It was a mistake you made, you should have hired a glamour puss for the job.'

'Instead of which I presented her with a dream come true, and you say she's still not satisfied?'

'Sometimes she is and sometimes she isn't,' Lallie shrugged. 'She's old, Owen, and she's feeling insecure. She's still afraid she'll be put away, somewhere where she can't be of any use to anybody. She's either changing her mind or she can't make it up. She wants Jonty married—you and me married—that's why I went over to Jonty's today trying to get something concrete for her to bite on. I thought I might be able to get rid of one of her worries, settle her mind about one thing at least, and I couldn't even do that for her.'

'Come along.' Owen rose to his feet and pulled her up with him. 'It's cold here and you'll soon be dissolving in a puddle of your own misery. Did you take her Dorcas's letter?'

'I took in the packet of photographs and things showing all the arrangements for the coming event, the snaps of the house before and after it had been done up, the nursery before and after it had been decorated, the frilly cot, the pattern for the knitted shawl and the bits of pink ribbon and blue which are going to trim little white things according to sex, but I didn't give her the letter, I read most of it out to her. Dorcas had forgotten to ask after her.'

'Too taken up with approaching motherhood,' after he grinned down at her as he led her towards the garden path. 'Dwynwen would have understood that, you silly thing.'

'Something else I've done wrong!' Out in the open air, some of Lallie's depression was evaporating.

'Not at all, just a small error in judgment.'

'It comes of having a sensitive nature myself,' she was rapidly regaining her normal tartness. 'I feel for others.'

'Tender-hearted little Lallie,' he mocked. 'Then start feeling for me. I'm hungry and I want my tea—or does your super-sensitive little soul exclude me, the arch-villain of the piece?'

She put her nose in the air and came in fighting. 'For those who need it, I'm all consideration. Work the rest out for yourself!'

'Mmm, I know you'd cheerfully watch me starve to death, wouldn't you? But please remember, I'm employing you as a stand-in housekeeper, the fact that you're supposed to be the light of my life and the darling of my heart doesn't apply. It's your business to see I'm fed, it's what you're drawing a very large salary for.'

'Now that's the first time I've heard anything about a salary, large or otherwise,' she retorted.

'Enlighten me, please. Who negotiated this enormous wage and who agreed to it?'

'Knowing you'd never agree to anything, not with
me—you'd have thrown my offer back in my face
and very likely spat in it at the same time—I negotiated with myself. Three and a half thousand a year,
less your keep—one half day off a week and holidays
at my discretion and convenience.'

'That's slave labour!' she gasped with outrage.
'Have you any idea of what I earned in London? *And*
with a thirty-five-hour week and four or five weeks'
holiday a year!'

The arm which had been hauling her up the crazy
paving tightened about her, bringing her to a full
stop. 'It's about right for full-time domestic staff, I
might even have erred on the generous side.'

'But in London . . .'

'In London,' he interrupted silkily, 'there, you
were exercising your talents, or at least one of them,
you were doing a job for which you'd been trained, at
which you were an expert—whereas here,' he paused
reflectively, 'you could say you're serving an appren-
ticeship. You're learning to run a house—the domestic side of your education was sadly neglected when
you were young—but you're not making a bad job of
it. I should think that in another few months you'll
be worth at least half of what I pay you, but I don't
complain.'

'I shouldn't think you would,' she flared. 'When I
think what I have to do, the hours I work . . .'

'Poor little thing—but as I was going to say when
you so rudely interrupted—your sweetly gentle voice
and your loving little gestures are worth every penny

I've been paying into the bank for you and I don't grudge a farthing of it.'

Lallie hid an expression of relief. Somehow, the idea of having a definite position in the house, even if it was only temporary, meant a lot to her. She was being employed here, she wasn't existing on his charity, and it pleased her enormously.

She recalled a discussion she had once had with the Whitechapel lady. They had been talking about appreciation and Lallie had said how much it meant to her, how it made the work seem worth while. She had been rather surprised at the lady's views.

'The only real appreciation is the size of your salary,' she had told Lallie. 'I know it sounds cynical, but it's true. Kind words, thanks and compliments don't mean a thing, they don't cost anything and they wouldn't even buy you a new pair of tights!'

At that time, it had sounded very mercenary to Lallie's naïve understanding, but now, she was more than ready to admit, there was something in what the Whitechapel lady had said.

'Thank you, Owen,' she murmured, then her belligerence reared its head again. 'But don't think you've bought me body and soul. I'd have done it without pay, you know that.'

'Mmm.' He whistled the collie, who obediently slunk into its kennel, and Owen paused with his hand on the latch of the back door porch. 'Another negotiation, while we're about it. Three months' notice on either side?'

'One month,' she bargained.

'Too little,' he countered. 'I'd need longer than

that to find a replacement. Two months?' and at her nod, 'Let's seal the bargain,' and his mouth swooped down on to hers, hesitating only for a second as he whispered, 'Make it look good, there's somebody watching.'

Lallie made it look good, although as she afterwards confessed to herself, she personally had nothing to do with it. It was as if there was somebody else inside her, a somebody who was hungry for kisses, who made her body soften and come alive against his so that, just for a few seconds, her lips parted willingly under his, her eyes closed and she couldn't get close enough to him. Jonty's old anorak which she was wearing, her clothes, his jacket and shirt, they were all in the way. She wanted to feel his skin against her own, slide her fingers over it and hold him to her, not let him get away.

She sighed as she felt her breasts harden against the cotton of her shirt, and she felt neither shame nor embarrassment when Owen's hand came to caress their pointed fulness. Later on she would; she knew that, but just at present she'd joined that despised seventy-five per cent of the female population, and she was enjoying it thoroughly so that when he raised his head and his mouth was no longer a hot demand against her own, she felt cold as though something wonderful and beautiful had been taken away from her.

'Inside.' Owen pushed her through the inner door into the kitchen just in time for her to see the door into the hall close quietly.

'Who?' she heard her voice shaking.

'How do I know?' he said indifferently. 'Nerys

perhaps, or Stella.' He stood for a moment, holding her by the shoulders and looking into her eyes seriously, then his mouth curved into the old mocking smile.

'You won't believe this, Lallie, but we're not as unalike as you like to think. We have the same basic drive,' and as she opened her mouth to protest, he slapped at her rear end. 'Tea now, there's a good girl, we'll talk later.'

It couldn't have been Nerys, Lallie worked that out as she went upstairs to wash and change into something a little more respectable than jeans and a tee-shirt—Nerys' bicycle had been gone from the back door and she thought she had seen the glimmer of the girl's gay flowered nylon overall hanging from its usual peg behind the kitchen door.

And she knew instinctively that it hadn't been Dwynwen. Dwynny could certainly get that far with her walking aid, but she would never venture into the kitchen, not while Stella was in the house and Lallie was out of it. Therefore it must have been Stella, unless Owen had been indulging in one of his twists of humour. She frowned at her reflection in the bathroom mirror. Somehow, she didn't mind either Nerys or Dwynwen seeing her making a fool of herself, but Stella was another matter.

When she came downstairs to prepare tea, she was neat and clean in her black pleated skirt and the second of Owen's cashmere twinsets, the gold one, which glowed against the black of her skirt. Her slim legs looked their best in cobwebby tights and the high-heeled black patent pumps and she hoped she hadn't overdone her make-up. She had felt in need of confidence and it was remarkable what a bit of powder and eye-shadow could do.

At twenty-six, she was no longer a naïve young girl, the one who had gone off to London full of determination to succeed. True, her experience was strictly limited, mainly to the behaviour of the odd boy-friend, but there were no longer any stars in her eyes. They had all been wiped out in the glare of unpleasant publicity, and after that she had been approached mostly by men who had read the papers and decided she was an easy touch. It had bred a cynicism in her and also an awareness of danger. She knew very well the feel of the hot demand of a man's body against her own, and there had been that demand in Owen's this afternoon.

Carefully she controlled a weak desire to burst into tears—she had been a bit generous with mascara and the damn stuff would run! She was wondering what Owen had in mind. He had said before that he could have her any time he wanted; she hadn't completely believed him then, but she believed him now.

But a mere sexual relationship wasn't good enough for her, it wouldn't satisfy. She had the depressing thought that what she felt would probably last for the rest of her life, that she'd never get over it, not completely.

She wiped any thought of marriage from her mind. Owen, she was almost sure, was too fastidious to take what he looked on as another man's leavings to wife, and she wouldn't have him if he was being pressured into it by Dwynwen. That would be worse than anything, worse than nothing. To live with a man she loved but who didn't love her—lots of girls might have settled for that sort of thing, but not Lallie Moncke.

She couldn't stand it, to see him off on one of his so called veterinary conferences—to watch his face when he came back—sniff to see whether the perfume on his clothes was her own or somebody else's—that way she'd end up a suspicious nagging bitch, impossible to live with.

Her face as she sat down at the table behind the teapot was set in a little mask of pleasantly quiet lines which admirably covered her inner turmoil, and she carefully paid no attention to Stella, who seemed a bit prickly. As soon as possible she escaped, going into Dwynwen's sitting room to pick up the empty tea-tray.

Dwynwen, her plate cleared down to the last crumb, was practising locomotion with her walking aid, but when Lallie entered, she put it away in a corner and sat down for a chat. She was still in her blue woollen dressing gown because dressing properly was out of the question until she could manage her corsets, and she looked up with a stern light in her eyes.

'Enjoy your tea?' Lallie made light conversation.

Dwynwen took note of the forced smile. 'What are you looking so sour about? Lost a shilling and picked up sixpence?'

'Nothing as bad as that,' Lallie smiled, and let the smile grow. 'I've been promoted, though. I'm now the official stand-in housekeeper—I'm even being paid a salary!'

Dwynwen sniffed; it wasn't what she wanted

to hear. 'You've been out this afternoon—over to Jonty's?'

'Mmm,' Lallie nodded, but at the eager enquiry in Dwywen's sharp eyes she shook her head. 'No news, I'm afraid.'

'But the lambing's over, or nearly so.' Owen had come in unnoticed, his pigskin casuals making no sound. He put a careless arm around Lallie's shoulders and smiled down at the old lady enigmatically. 'They might have more time now for the less important things of life.'

'Bah!' Dwynwen was not to be diverted. 'Less important things indeed! There's nothing so important as living a good, pure life.'

'They could be doing just that,' Owen pointed out humorously. 'Perhaps it's all in your mind, Dwynwen. After all, you haven't a scrap of evidence, I believe you listen to gossip!'

Dwynwen didn't rise to the bait—ordinarily she would have given him the length of her tongue, but now she sat silent, looking defeated. Then her old head reared erect, like a cobra striking. 'And when are you two going to get married?' she demanded with asperity.

Owen's arm tightened about Lallie's shoulders, his fingers closing on her upper arm without mercy. 'In about three weeks' time,' he drawled. There was something in his manner which made Lallie think it would be unwise to contradict him, so she remained silent. 'Stella will be in her hotel by then, superintending the last touches,' he continued smoothly. 'That'll leave Lallie free for other things, and we don't want another scandal in the family, do we?' He made himself sound virtuous. 'One's enough!'

Dwynwen's face cleared. 'Glad to hear it,' she muttered, and then, as if she needed justification, ''Bout time too. Oh, go on, get out of here. I want to get on with my walking practice, and you've got something better to do than stand here talking to an old woman!'

CHAPTER EIGHT

BACK in the kitchen, Owen whirled on Lallie before she could open her mouth, pushing her into the rocking chair and standing over it, his face set and hard.

'Explode quietly,' he advised. 'I don't want a noisy row.'

'If that's your idea of a joke,' she struggled against his hands while kicking out at his knees, 'I'm not amused!'

'Nobody asked you to laugh your head off,' he snapped, 'but that's the way it's going to be, you can take it from me. I'm doing the best I know for this damn' family of mine and you aren't going to stop me!'

Lallie stopped struggling and kicking; from somewhere she found some dignity. 'I'm not going to marry you, Owen—not in three weeks, three years or thirty. Don't be any more of a fool than you are already, it won't work and you know it.'

'I'm not a fool, my girl, and it *will* work.' He was supremely confident.

'You can't make me,' she pointed out reasonably. 'You could perhaps tie me up, drag me off to the church, but unless you gagged me, you couldn't stop me from saying "No".' She had a vivid mental picture of herself, trussed up like a chicken, gagged and very mute, and it made her giggle almost hysterically. 'I couldn't say "Yes" either.'

'I can make you do anything I want,' he wasn't smiling at her feeble little joke. 'I think I've proved that already, and I've only been coasting. Wait till I get into top gear.' Lallie closed her eyes and shivered at the thought, and he shook her till her head felt as though it would drop off.

'Listen to me,' he stopped shaking her. 'I told you, we have the same basic drive, you and I, we'll do very well for each other. You've gone your own road this last eight years and it hasn't been all that rosy for you, has it? No, don't try to tell me you've enjoyed every moment of it, because I wouldn't believe you if you swore it on a stack of bibles.' He watched her wag her head at him and a grim smile started to play about his firm mouth. 'Now you'll go mine, Lallie, for a while at least; it won't be a hard road and I'll help you over the bad bits. Oh, I see what it is,' as she continued to wag her head. 'You want the pretty words, the sugar on the pill. Come off it, girl, you've been away a hell of a time, you're twenty-six and you've been around—you know exactly how much those words are worth, you've heard them before.'

As usual, his almost bitter condemnation robbed her of words and her eyes filled with tears. She didn't want pretty words. As he said, she'd heard them before, enough of them to know their worth. All she wanted was for him to believe her—believe in her, not to think she was the promiscuous little tramp she'd been made out to be.

And part of it was her own fault, that was what was making her cry. Her damn tongue, she admitted to herself miserably. When she lost her temper, when she was pushed right at the edge, it ran away with her and she'd let it run with a vengeance. Oh yes, she wanted love, but over and above that, she wanted, needed respect. One without the other was no good.

'Three weeks.' Owen looked at her enigmatically, quite unmoved by her obvious distress. 'I want your word on that—and hurry up, *cariad*, or I'll make it three days!'

'No!' It burst from her as a host of thoughts started up and began running at top speed through her brain. Three days! Stella wouldn't have gone by then, and that she couldn't bear. Not to come down in the morning to see those pale blue eyes looking at her, dissecting her and becoming filled with a private knowledge. Because Stella would know, she *had* been there before!

'Three weeks,' she agreed huskily, 'but it won't work, Owen. It's all built on lies and deceit.'

'What lies, what deceit?' Now that she had agreed, now he was sure of getting his own way, he lost a lot of his menace and became more human and reasonable. 'I'm telling no lies and neither are you, so where's the deceit? You'll stay here and be a model wife, curb your nasty little temper and keep your eyes off other men—and don't think you'll be able to skip off just when the fancy takes you, because I won't let you. In a year's time, *cariad*, you'll be wondering what you made all the fuss about.'

'All this to keep Dwynny happy!' Lallie said drearily, and was surprised at his response.

'Dwynwen's only a side issue, my girl, although I admit that what she wants does have a small bearing on things, but that's because the old lady's got more sense than you credit her with, and in any case, we all owe her a lot. She spent a great many years of her life caring for you little ones, you and Jonty and Dorcas—she deserves to spend the rest of her time in comfort and security—but as I said, she's really only a side issue. I'm doing what I think best for all of us—you, me, Jonty and Dwynwen.'

'Jonty as well?' Lallie raised a supercilious eyebrow. 'My, Owen! You seem to have everybody's welfare at heart, and it's such a big heart, isn't it? We all have to go your way, don't we, because as always, you know best.' Her mouth twisted bitterly. 'Do you think that once Jonty sees how blissfully happy we are, what an aura of domestic felicity we live in, he'll at last get the message and go and do likewise? A fine example we'll be—you despise me and I hate you, all the acting in the world won't cover that up. In any case, I think it's Vi who's holding back.'

'And I might believe you, but I'm taking no chances. I hoped the poor young devil was over you, I believed he was, but now I'm not so sure any longer so I'm going to make certain. Once you and I are married, he'll be able to put any thoughts about you and him out of his mind, I'm almost sure the thoughts do linger.'

'Nonsense!' she flared.

'No, it's not, not from where I'm standing,' there was a rueful gleam in Owen's eyes. 'You caught him young, *cariad*, and I think he might be still dazzled, although as you say, it might be Vi who's hanging back. But again, if she is, why? Could it be that she's the same as the rest of us, waiting to see which way you'll jump? He's probably bored her to tears with his talk about you and she might be worried that if it came to a choice, he'd choose you.'

'You're out of your mind!' Lallie's temper was rising. 'We've seen each other once since I came back, and that time he hardly spoke to me.'

'No, but he watched you and Vi watched him watching you and I watched Vi watching him watching you. Never mind, in a few months' time, when he sees the bad-tempered little shrew you've become, when it gets through to him that I'm a henpecked husband, he'll probably start counting his blessings. Then Vi will have him and another problem will be solved.'

'Leaving just you and me.'

'No problem there,' he smiled smugly. 'I can handle you, Lallie, with one hand tied behind my back. Of course, I shall give the impression of being a downtrodden husband, but you and I, we'll know who's the boss, won't we?' It was a definite threat, and she contemplated the future with a jaundiced eye.

'It's going to be hell,' she sighed.

'Only during the daylight hours,' he comforted, 'we'll make the nights enjoyable. Now, make some coffee and I'll fetch the whisky—we'll have a drink to celebrate this happy occasion. Are you going to insist on a white wedding?'

Lallie didn't ignore the last question, she merely put it aside. She knew the answer to that one, she was determined on it! A white wedding—and why not? She was entitled, wasn't she? Let Owen and the rest of them sneer, she'd wear white just to spit in his eyes! Instead of saying this, she roused herself to make a suggestion.

'When you're fetching the whisky, you'd better ask Stella to join us.'

'Stella?' He looked at her as though she'd gone out of her mind. 'Stella went down to her sister's directly after tea. What else did you expect after that convincing little act we put on outside the back door?'

So that had been an act as well. Tears came in a hard lump in Lallie's throat so that she found herself swallowing with difficulty.

'Quite a performance, wasn't it?' she croaked. 'I think we did very well for an off-the-cuff, spur-of-the-moment thing.'

'That's right. You see, another little problem solved and no bones broken.'

No bones, only hearts—and Lallie's heart wept as she spooned coffee into the percolater and set cups on the table, but she fought back her tears and maintained a stolid front; she even scraped up a bit of humour from some last reserve.

'It's the transition.' She heard Owen coming back, the bottle and glasses chinking, and she hurried into an explanation for her lack of enthusiasm.

'At four o'clock this afternoon, I was a working girl, a housekeeper with a good position and a modest salary to make up for the lack of prospects. Now I'm a bride-to-be. What's going to happen to that salary?'

'It ceases, my mercenary little cat, as from your wedding day.' He came behind her and put a heavy hand on her shoulder and she let it stay there, she was too tired to shrug it off.

'Can't we fix things some other way?' There was desperation in her voice. 'There's the Parry cottage, Owen, it's been empty since Mr Parry died and his wife went to live with her daughter. Couldn't we have it, Dwynwen and I? I'll take care of her . . .'

'And what good would that do?' His hand dropped from her shoulder and went to her hip, pulling her back against him so that the coffee percolater was slightly out of her reach. She watched the fountain of water bubbling up into the transparent dome, trying to find some spark of life within herself, but there was none; she felt drained and dead.

'My way's best, Lallie.'

'When wasn't it ever?' she answered dully. 'You're a grand one at manipulation, you manipulate everybody. Oh, I know—I remember what you said, in about a year we'll be wondering what I was getting so worked up about, but don't you see—it's all no good, it won't work.'

'It wasn't necessary to manipulate everybody, my sweet, only you.' She thought she felt him laugh. 'You've always been the quiet, sneaky sort.' This time she heard the laugh, short and hard. 'Whenever trouble broke out, I only had to look a little deeper than the surface to find you at the bottom of it—yet you always managed to get round everybody. You created quite a stir in London, but immediately, Jonty and Dwynwen were hot in your defence—he said outright that he didn't believe it of you and I practically had to tie him down to stop him charging to your rescue, and Dwynwen said you should be forgiven, that you were young and that every girl could be forgiven one mistake, men being what they are!'

'But not in your book!' Lallie wrenched herself free and took the coffee pot to the table, sitting down to pour it out and looking glumly at the two whisky glasses, each with a couple of inches of golden liquid. She seized her own and drained it at a gulp, but there was no instant lift of her spirits and the famous glow turned out to be a hot rawness in her throat that made her splutter. The whisky didn't do a thing for her.

'That's no way to treat a single malt!' Owen reproved. 'Cheer up, girl, it's not the end of the world. Drink your coffee and trot on, off to bed—you'll feel better in the morning.'

'Just what I intend to do—and you can take in Dwynwen's night time drink and her pills, and you can also get your own supper.' She halted at the kitchen door. 'You won't be told, will you? Well, you'll just have to learn for yourself. I'll do what you want, but you'll regret it, I promise you that!' and with a defiant fling, she was through the door to bang it noisily behind her.

Her feet carried her upstairs unwillingly and along the passage to the bedroom. She was wasting valuable talking time; Owen wasn't going to let her have her say. She would therefore do what he wanted and not because he was driving her into it. She made a face at the mirror. She would do it because she was as weak as water and she wanted it that way. On impulse, she went back to the bedroom door and slammed that as well.

Once in bed, she lay awake thinking. Owen

wanted his own way and he should have it, so she left the grim prospect of the distant future out of her planning programme to concentrate upon immediates. When she had those settled in her mind, she turned on her side and drifted off to sleep, so that, in the morning, when she met him over the breakfast table, she was composed and calm.

'I have to go to London.' It wasn't a request but a plain statement of fact.

'Why?'

'Immoral purposes, of course,' she hissed. 'Isn't that what you expect?' and then her tone changed to one of ice. 'I want to see about my flat, my rent's due at the end of April and I may as well give it up. There's no point in keeping it on, not now.'

'You can do that by phone,' he pointed out reasonably.

'Ugh-ugh,' she shook her head. 'There are some things I left there, clothes and personal items, and I want them.'

'Such as?'

'Like I said, my clothes. There aren't many, but I don't see the sense of abandoning them, and there are some photographs and books, my portable typewriter and the desk it stands on . . .'

'I'll take you this weekend,' he offered, and she choked on his magnanimity.

'No "conference", Owen? My! You *are* the liberated man!'

'And that's something you'd better start learning to control,' he glowered at her. 'Your tongue—it's a pretty deadly weapon.'

Fortunately, Stella's advent stopped a full-scale

quarrel. Lallie simmered down while she made fresh toast and Owen told Stella the news. Stella took it very well, considering.

'All the best, Owen, and congratulations to you, Lallie.' Her smile was tight and Lallie wondered if the turn-round of the phrases had been deliberate. It was she who should have been wished well, but Stella was evidently not one to weep over spilled milk, being more of an 'off with the old and on with the new' type, and Lallie realised for the first time that she'd never been jealous of Stella. She hadn't liked her, but there had never been anything of jealousy in it, merely envy at an appearance and sophistication which she herself could never achieve.

It was as though she had known from the moment they met that Owen had no long-term arrangements for Stella; she wasn't right for him, he knew it and Lallie had known he knew it. All her dislike had stemmed from Stella's treatment of Dwynwen, nothing else, and if she had made capital out of Owen with her 'your Stella', there had been no jealousy involved. She brought the fresh toast to the table with a pleasant smile and sat down feeling much better.

'How big's the desk?' That was Owen harking back to what he considered the basics.

'Quite small,' she sketched with her hands. 'About three foot by a little more than one and a half and the usual height. Why?'

'Could we get it on the back seat of the Bentley, or would we need the Land Rover? Is it heavy?'

'No, not very,' she buttered toast reflectively, 'and I think it would go in the Bentley, upside down. I bought it about fifteenth-hand, and it didn't cost much, but I liked it, it's a pretty little desk. I'd like to keep it if I can.' Mentally, she crossed her fingers hoping she was right and that it would go in the car. The thought of a journey to London and back in the hard-sprung Land Rover wasn't to her taste and beside, she was feeling a bit battered and delicate, too delicate for the Land Rover.

'All right, this weekend we can fix up with Mrs Parry to stay with Dwynwen, they'll talk their heads off and be quite happy.'

'Thanks.' She was meagre with her gratitude— but then why should she be generous? It was all being done for his benefit, not hers! She smiled nicely, while one part of her was filled with the evil hope that Jonty and Vi would continue in their irregular relationship for years and years—that would learn him!

The narrow Victorian house looked narrower and more cramped to Lallie's eyes as she looked at it from the car window. It looked like a shabby, down-at-heel matron, but she shrugged the thought aside. It was just the contrast with Bryn Celyn where everything was well maintained, where the paint always looked fresh. There was nothing run-down about that house despite its great age; Owen thought too much of his home to allow it to grow shabby.

The landlady was surprised to see her. She seemed a little offended, but Lallie put it right. 'I'm leaving at the end of the month,' she smiled at the woman. 'What I really mean is, I'm giving up my tenancy as from April the thirtieth. I'll pay you a month's rent in lieu of notice, of course.' She stood there in the hall, waiting for Owen, who was coming up the steps with a picnic basket she'd packed specially for the occasion.

'We'll need something to eat when we get there, or at least a cup of tea,' she had explained. 'So we'll have to take a few things. There'll be gas, but I rang when I knew I was staying at Bryn Celyn and the landlady will have cleared out the fridge and anything perishable. You can make us a drink while I sort things out and we'll go to a restaurant for a meal when I've done.'

'We can take in a show, if you like.' She had marvelled at his good temper; he hardly ever called her a vicious little bitch now, just sometimes it was there in his eyes, that suppressed anger, but she ignored it. She was practising for the future which had to be made tolerable.

Upstairs, she looked in her kitchenette and wondered how she had ever managed in such a confined space, before she went back into the lobby to feed a few coins into the gas meter. Coming back into the living room, she frowned at the narrow divan.

'Have you made arrangements for tonight?' she asked.

'Two rooms in a hotel in Islington—everything very proper, Lallie, so don't start suspecting my motives,' and he went off to the kitchenette to put the kettle on while she started opening drawers and cupboards.

'I'm not bothering with the pots and pans,' she called through to him. 'The next tenant can have them with my good wishes. Oh dear, I didn't realise there were so many things I'd want to keep.

'Is the desk too big?' she asked as they sat by the gas fire drinking tea and eating ham sandwiches.

'Go on the back seat easily.' Owen measured it with his eye. 'You're right, it is a pretty thing, we'll have to find somewhere for it.'

'I thought of putting it in the window embrasure in the sitting room.' Lallie was talking, they were both talking just for the sake of something to do, she realised that, and her heart fell. Was this how it was going to be for the rest of her life? Speaking, saying words, words that meant nothing—no real tie between them? Without thinking very much and with her eyes fixed on the glow of the fire, she thought back aloud.

'I was quite happy here, I used to think of it as a kind of fortress, when I was up here. I was out of touch, away from everything. Those people you put me with,' she smiled, 'isn't it odd, I can't even remember what they were called. I didn't like it there. I know they were probably doing what they thought was best for me, you know—in by ten every evening, nice substantial meals, but all the time, the idea in my head that I was being watched, distrusted. I felt as though I was being reclaimed or something like that. I wouldn't have been in the least surprised if they'd prayed over me.'

'Good for you,' he said unsympathetically, 'it gave you a chance to learn some self-discipline, and you never had very much of that, *cariad*.'

'No,' she chuckled. 'I didn't, did I? I must have been a foul little monster.'

'I'm glad you realise what I had to put up with.' Owen helped himself to another sandwich from Dwynwen's treasured picnic basket.

'Oh, I wasn't as bad as all that, and when I came here it was wonderful—the relief of having somewhere of my own, not being supervised. It didn't go to my head, though.'

'You had a rough time, but you learned from it, I hope.'

'Oh yes, I learned.' She kept her eyes on the fire as though she was looking back at those days. 'I used to think everybody was looking at me, talking about me—I nearly developed a complex about it until I realised that most of them didn't know me from Adam and that those who did recognise me couldn't care less whether I was alive or dead. It was something the same with the papers as well. After a while, they were just newspapers, no good on the day after except to wrap up the rubbish in—it was the letters that offended me most.'

'Letters?' He prodded her on gently.

'Mmm, I had quite a lot. You know the thing, "Betrayed Wife in Wimbledon", "Abandoned Wife in Streatham", that type of letter—anybody would have thought I was personally responsible for every broken marriage in the country! There were a few others from men,' she giggled. 'Most of them contained proposals of marriage—some men have the kinkiest ideas!'

She heard Owen grunt and went silent while her thoughts took another direction. She'd never thought of this solution before, it wasn't what she wanted, but then neither was what he proposed, but if she was to be unhappy for the rest of her life, did it matter?

'Owen,' she began hesitantly while she put her ideas into a logical sequence, 'you know I'm not happy with your way of doing things?' She waited for some response, even if it was only another grunt, but none was forthcoming.

'I've just thought of something, I can't think why it didn't occur to me before . . .'

'Another hare-brained scheme?' Owen didn't sound very co-operative—but then, she consoled herself, he wasn't thinking as far ahead as she was and he was so blandly sure that he could cope and that she could cope . . . oh hell!

'There's no need for us to get married.' She was bald about it, there had been just the one way of saying it and she'd taken it. She went on swiftly before he could stop her.

'We needn't, not really. Look, this is Friday and we arrived here just after two, we're going back either tomorrow night or Sunday—that's right, isn't it? Why can't we come down again next weekend or even the one after, stay for the same amount of time and go back to tell them we were married at some London register office. You could say you got the licence today while I was packing my things up. Nobody would ever know, and then after a while, when Dwynny's all brand new, I can come back to London.

'Don't you see,' she raised her head to look at his uncommunicative face, 'it'll save a lot of bother later on. We won't have to go through a real divorce if we don't have a real marriage, and in two years or so,

I'm not all sure about the time required, you could be as free as air, all your worries over, Jonty nicely settled, Dwynwen back on her feet, and I'll slide gently and gracefully out of the picture.' She gave a weak chuckle. 'I can't think why I didn't think of it before, it's the perfect solution. I could dress up a bit, we could have a photograph taken . . .' Her voice faltered into silence.

Owen put his cup and saucer on the floor and stood up, drawing her up with him. His arm went round her while his free hand tangled in the hair at her nape, forcing her face upwards. When his mouth found hers, she struggled weakly and then relaxed, giving away to the sweetness of it, the warmth, the demand, until she felt as though she was floating.

Without any conscious thought on her part, her hands went to his head to thread through the hair and hold him to her, her lips parted under his and she felt his whole body tauten and harden demandingly against her. When he finally raised his head from hers, she was trembling and her face wore a drugged look, her eyelids too heavy to lift to look at him.

'And what do we do about that?' His harsh voice broke the spell. 'Are you going to live in sin with me, Lallie?'

'S-stop sounding so old-fashioned!' she was almost crying. 'Of course not, but we can pretend, can't we? We're alone in the house, who's to know any different? A b-business arrangement, strictly business, that's all.'

The shake he gave her wasn't violent, more the

sort he would have given a puppy which had only slightly misbehaved itself.

'You said my way wasn't right, that it wouldn't work,' he reminded her. 'You said it couldn't work, it was founded on lies and deceit, but compared to what you've just suggested, it was a shining example of honesty. No, my dear, we do it my way.'

'But it isn't necessary!' She pushed against him, trying to free herself. 'It's all a pretence,' she muttered dully, 'an outward show. I know you think you're right, but you're not, you're only laying up more trouble, and by the time you've finished, it'll be so deep I'll never be able to get out from under.'

'Scared, Lallie?'

'You're so right, Owen, I'm scared. I've been running my own life for too long now to toss into somebody else's keeping with a lighthearted laugh. You stifle me!'

'Not you,' he disagreed. 'Just a few of your less lovable tendencies, like your bitter little tongue and your predeliction for middle-aged men.'

'I knew you'd get round to that some time.' She wasn't miserable now, she was furious. 'So you don't think I'm a lily of purity—well, I don't think you're so stain-free either. Tit for tat!'

'That's better,' he laughed in her face. 'I don't like it when you get morbid. Stop looking so far ahead, you can leave that to me. Now, find yourself something nice to wear this evening and put it where you can get at it easily, I don't want to have to rake everything out of the boot because you've forgotten where you put your shoes or something.'

So she could leave it to him, could she? Her eyes

sparked with a small fury. 'I shall do some shopping tomorrow morning,' she announced as firmly as she knew how. 'I shall buy a wedding dress. White!'

CHAPTER NINE

STELLA went off to her hotel, leaving her last little barbed remarks sticking in Lallie's tender flesh.

'I do *hope* you'll be happy.' Stella made it sound as though it was so improbable, it was an impossibility. Lallie didn't think it was probable either, but she put on a brave front.

'I'll work at it,' she murmured with the ghost of a smile.

'Mmm.' Stella gave her the complete head-to-foot inspection which made her feel desperately inadequate. 'Of course, with Owen knowing all about you,' the *all* was very gently stressed, 'you won't have to worry overmuch about bones in the closet, will you? Although in your shoes, I'd be more inclined to run than stay. Men can be very unfair, and that's the sort of thing that gets thrown in a girl's face during the first quarrel!' Stella crossed her legs and contemplated the toe of one shoe. 'You're a fairly efficient housekeeper and with the proper sort of training, you could be a good cook.'

'I'll come to you for a reference.' Lallie painted a smile on her face.

'Or a job.' Stella looked businesslike. 'I like to have an efficient staff, as you know, and you'd soon learn my ways,' she shrugged. 'Don't turn up your nose at the offer, I mean it, and you could always look on it as a lifeline. You might need one.'

Lallie walked down the garden path with Stella, saw her off in her little car and went back to the house with the feeling that one problem had been solved. Now there was only Dwynwen who was enjoying a bad-tempered convalescence and had been bitten with a spring-cleaning bug.

'Not a fresh bit of wallpaper or a lick of paint anywhere,' she grumbled as she sat in her chair and seethed with impotence.

'It was all done last year,' Lallie soothed, pointing out three errors in the latest of Dwynwen's interminable games of Patience.

'I almost wish she was a proper invalid again,' she grumbled to Owen later. 'She was much easier to manage!'

In an odd way, she and Owen were getting on much better now that she had accepted her fate with the proper degree of meekness. He seemed almost amused at her infrequent outbursts of temper, contenting himself with a smile of lordly condescension at the worst excesses of her cutting tongue.

'Get Mrs Parry up to stay with her,' he advised. 'She's coming up the night before the wedding and I expect she'll be quite glad to come a few days early. I hear her grandchildren are driving her up the wall.' He grimaced and became very Welsh. 'No doing anything with children nowadays, no proper discipline or respect?'

Mrs Parry came and things became better. Now, the two old ladies sat in Dwynwen's room, drinking endless cups of nearly black tea from Dwynwen's rose-spattered china and reminiscing about their days in service, which gave Lallie a chance to escape down to Aber where a dressmaker was altering her wedding dress.

She had bought it in London, the best she could afford out of her own money; she hadn't even used any of the salary he'd paid her. Owen was sardonic about that dress, mostly about its whiteness, and not a penny of Tudor money would she spend on it. So it was an off-the-peg effort that didn't fit very well—too long, too wide, but the dressmaker had been encouraging.

'It suits you, or it would if it fitted—the simple line is what you need, full skirts and wide sleeves would make you look dumpy. I'll take it apart and re-cut it.' And now Lallie was on her way to Aber, by bus from Trellwyd, which meant a walk down to the village, up the Nant which was a short cut that cut off at least a mile and a half—a nice walk if one had the time and energy for it. The Nant was a steep little hill.

Lallie had allowed herself the time, but she hadn't a lot of energy. This last week she had dropped into a state of depression where there was no glimmer of joy or sunshine, no hope, no anything. But at least, walking like this, she was on her own and no longer had to put on a false face. She didn't have to smile or be full of joy for anybody's benefit.

Once or twice she had wondered if her wedding night would change Owen's opinion of her, but she doubted it. He'd be far more likely to either ignore it or to think she was putting on an act. Whatever happened, she was in the position of 'heads, Owen wins—tails, Lallie loses', but then she'd been on a losing streak ever since Owen had turned up in her flat and dragged her back here to Bryn Celyn.

The bus from Trellwyd dropped her at the terminus in Aber which was situated just outside the railway station. She looked at it with longing eyes, but running away wasn't something she normally did, and in any case, it needed a bit of planning. She glanced down at her tee-shirt and jeans, covered by Jonty's old anorak, and then at her sandalled feet. She might look like a hippy, but she wasn't one. Wherever she went, she'd require a change of clothes and somewhere to sleep—more important, she'd require a job to keep her, and since she'd given up her flat, she had none of these things. All she had was a pair of white satin slippers and a long white nylon slip in her shoulder bag.

'You've done a wonderful job.' She pirouetted before the long mirror in the dressmaker's workroom. The dress looked very nice and even a scrappy lunch in a milk bar couldn't make her feel quite so bad. The dress had been remade, and the total effect was that it fitted nicely in all the right places and looked far more expensive than it really was. It was understated, and on Lallie that looked good.

The dressmaker shrugged. 'Anything looks better when it fits. I'm quite pleased with it myself. Do you want to take it with you?'

'Not just now,' Lallie made up her mind swiftly. 'I'll finish off my shopping and call back for it—is that all right?'

She didn't have much to do, so she walked along the Promenade, looking at the sea, and then called for the dress just before going into the one cinema. She wouldn't see all the performance, the last bus for Trellwyd left the terminus too early for that, but the film watching was only a method of delaying her return and it was an excellent way of passing the time, sitting in the darkness and paying little attention to a space epic which was colourful, predictable and incredibly noisy. So that when she left the bus at Trellwyd, her head was still spinning with the noise of the film and her problems which she had hashed and rehashed all the way from Aber. The dressbox was a weight in her arms and her problems were a weight on her heart.

If only Owen had agreed to her proposal in London—she would never be able to understand why he hadn't. It would have been the most wonderful get-out, everything under control and no waves, not even a ripple, with, at the end of a couple of years, all the loose ends tidied away with nothing to show it had ever happened—and nobody hurt. This way, somebody was going to be hurt, and she rather thought it would be herself.

The street lighting showed her the Land Rover parked at the kerbside and Owen lounging against the door, so, clutching her box, Lallie walked towards him.

'Waiting for me?' she asked pertly. 'How kind and thoughtful of you!'

'And where have you been all day?' He sounded dangerously bad-tempered.

'Out,' she answered briefly. 'What's the matter, did you miss me?'

'Like a cold in the head,' he was equally brief. 'But you should have told somebody where you were going. I came home to a houseful of hens all clucking about not knowing where you were.'

'I've been to the dress-maker's, and on the way I looked longingly at the railway station, but as you see,' she gestured at her jeans and anorak, 'I wasn't dressed for London.' She glanced at him sideways. 'Owen, I believe you've been worried, did you think I'd run out on you?'

'I wouldn't put it past you.' In the light of the street lamp, his smile glimmered. 'You've an ingrained habit of disobedience.'

'Only when I'm provoked,' she answered demurely, and then, as he took her box from her arms and tossed it over the seats and into the tarpaulined interior of the vehicle, 'Hey! That's my wedding dress! It's "handle with care", "this side up" and "don't drop".'

'You're in a merry mood!'

'Of course, why shouldn't I be? Here am I, little Lallie Moncke with nothing to recommend me but an awkward disposition, and I'm going to be married on Saturday to the local Don Juan who's also a wealthy vet. I've been congratulating myself on my good luck all day. A Cinderella story come true!'

'That's better.' She caught the glimmer of his teeth as his mouth stretched in a smile. 'You haven't been your usual caustic little self these past few days, I was thinking you were perhaps sickening for something.'

'Merely obeying orders,' she murmured. 'Keeping a low profile and a guard on my tongue.'

'Becoming used to the idea?'

'Resigned.' She gave a huge sigh. 'I walked along the prom today and contemplated suicide, but the water's too cold this time of year, I'll have to wait until it's warmer.'

'Cinderellas don't do things like that.' Owen put his hand under her elbow and steered her across the street.

'No, they don't, do they?' she muttered. 'They put on the glass slipper, smile widely and marry Prince Charming.' Suddenly she felt beaten as though all the fight had gone out of her again.

'I don't think the glass slipper fits this Cinderella, Owen. It's going to pinch my toes.'

'Then put on a smile to cover the pain,' he advised. 'Nobody's going to look that closely, only me. Come on, we'll go to the pub and have a drink.'

The interior of the pub was dim and smoke-filled, even in the lounge, and from the public bar came the sounds of a dart match with the accompanying thud of darts in the board and the whoops of delight and groans of anguish. Lallie sat quietly and sipped at half a pint of shandy.

'Jonty and Vi came over this evening.' Owen put his tankard down precisely in the middle of the beer mat. 'They hung on for quite a while, but they had to go. Something about a late lamb Vi's bottle-feeding.'

'Sorry,' she grimaced, 'but I didn't know. I went to the cinema when I'd finished my bit of shopping. How are they?'

'The usual,' he shrugged. 'They thanked us for the wedding invitation, brought a present, I've asked Jonty if he'd like to give you away—I can hardly do it myself.'

'Oh, I don't know.' She glanced at him speculatively. 'You could walk me up the aisle, do a quick sidestep when we get to the rails and take your place at my right hand.' She stopped suddenly to glance around, but the lounge was nearly empty, most people were watching the darts match and the few left in here were intent on their own conversations. 'If what you've told me is true, isn't that rather a cruel thing to do?'

Owen took a quick glance at her over the rim of his tankard. 'You talking about cruelty, Lallie? You went your careless, unheeding way without a thought for anybody's feelings.'

'Another area where we're totally compatible,' she shrugged, delving into a packet of crisps. 'You were right, Owen, we have so many things in common, I'm discovering new ones every day. I don't think I like myself very much!' The last words came out with a snap and a look of disgust.

Saturday morning dawned fine and clear, Lallie watched the sun rise from her bed, huddled under the clothes and feeling sick and shivery. Perhaps she'd caught a chill—she amplified it—a nice feverish one with complications—anything to stop this happening to her. She stifled a sob and then thought, why not? She was quite alone, there was nobody to see her, she could cry her head off if she wanted to. Weep for what she wanted but would never have, could never have—love instead of disdain, warmth and sweetness instead of a hot passion which would be wonderful but quite unsatisfactory.

Then she pulled herself together. Owen wasn't ever going to know how much she was hurt—she'd hidden that hurt before, she'd been doing a good job of hiding it for weeks now, and she was *not* going to walk down the aisle of the stone church in Trellwyd with puffy eyes! She pattered off to the bathroom to splash cold water in her face and then came back to bed.

As she lay there, waiting for seven o'clock, she made her resolutions. She would be a good wife for however long it lasted. She would cultivate her abominable tongue instead of suppressing it, and nobody should ever know she was dying inside— bleeding to death. The minutes dragged by on leaden feet, the hands of the bedside clock hardly seeming to move. She dozed a little and dreamed fantastic things until Nerys was there at the bedside with a laden tray and her usual vacuous smile.

'Nerys!' Lallie sat upright with a gasp. 'What are you doing here today? You're supposed to be having it off, going to the wedding.'

'Going,' Nerys said monosyllabically, then giggled as though she'd won the pools. 'Owen's taking me when he goes down—plenty of time. Came to give you your breakfast, Miss Roberts said I could.'

Lallie thought that one out. Dwynwen was Miss Roberts but Owen was just Owen as far as Nerys was concerned, and she wondered whether that was a good sign or not. Apparently Owen was a lot easier to approach than Dwynwen was; it bore thinking about. To her, Owen had represented authority and Dwynwen had been a friend, but Nerys saw it the other way round!

'Going down with Owen? You are in luck.' Lallie put on a cheerful face and a voice to match it.

'And having my photograph taken with him as well.' Pleasure and excitement made Nerys talkative. 'He said so—special, he called it, because you weren't having any bridesmaids.'

Lallie suddenly felt very mean and small-minded. She should have thought of something like this, some little thing which would have given the girl pleasure instead of wallowing in her own puddle of misery. To cover the moment, she looked at the tray and forced a smile.

'It looks lovely.' She eyed the brown egg nestling in its cup and the thin sticks of toast. 'We'll have to watch out or you'll be taking a job in a swish hotel where you're really appreciated!'

'Like it here,' Nerys shook her head. 'Nice and close to my mam,' and she disappeared through the open door.

Left with the tray, Lallie pulled the toast into crumbs and spread them on the windowsill. She was undecided what to do with the egg, so she wrapped it up in a couple of tissues and poked it in the toe of a pair of flat shoes she hardly ever wore, hoping she wouldn't forget it, she could dispose of it later—and then she drank the whole contents of the small teapot thirstily.

When she came back from the bathroom, it was to find Vi standing by the bed, a very elegant Vi in a silky, bronze-coloured two-piece and wearing a small hat of the same colour on her soft brown hair. She looked confident and capable, and Lallie nearly flew to her to weep on her shoulder. Hastily she recovered herself.

'Why, hello, Vi, do you think it's going to stay fine?'

'I hope so,' Vi smiled quietly. 'There's nothing

worse than a wet bride, is there? I've come to help, if I may . . .' She looked at Lallie seriously. 'I've plenty of experience, my mother remarried when I was nineteen and since then I've helped my two sisters when they were wed, so I know what to do. My mother was the worst, she was convinced it was going to be wet, she threw her hat on the floor—and talking about nerves, Jonty and Owen are downstairs, both of them pretending to be calm and collected.'

'Thanks,' Lallie said gratefully. 'I was wondering how I'd manage if my zip stuck—I could feel myself going into hysterics at the thought.'

'I'll calm them,' Vi told her soothingly, 'and I didn't come here just to help, you know. I've got a bit of news which maybe will take your mind off things, like Jonty and me. We've decided—that is, I've decided,' she handed Lallie the treasured pair of silk stockings and stood waiting with the long slip. 'I had to think about it and I'm sorry it took so long, but like I said, my mother remarried, a man younger than herself, and things didn't work out very well. I was afraid the same thing might happen to me. I'm older than Jonty, nearly five years.'

'Pooh!' Lallie struggled into the slip and when it was down over her head, her voice came out muffled by the folds. 'What's five years nowadays?' At last her head was free and she smiled widely. 'That's wonderful news, I hope you'll be very happy—and I'm not just saying that, I mean it.' It was amazing how thinking about somebody else took her mind off her own personal tragedy.

Vi stood with her back to Lallie and she muttered

as she lifted the dress from its hook. 'I was a bit worried about you as well,' she admitted. 'I knew Jonty'd had this thing about you when he was younger, and it wasn't until I saw you together that I knew it had died the death.'

'Sheer madness.' Lallie sat down on the bed and looked up. 'I never felt that way about him and I didn't know anything about it till Owen shoved it in my face. Jonty's always been like a brother, that's the only way I've ever thought of him.'

'But Owen wasn't a brother?' Vi teased.

'Owen was a tyrant,' Lallie glowered, and then remembered she was supposed to be happily in love with the tyrant. The emphasis was on 'happily'—the love was there, but she didn't think she'd have much joy from it. 'But don't you dare get married, not until Owen and I are back from wherever he's taking us.'

'And not until the sheepdog trials are over,' Vi laughed, a musical sound, understanding and happy. 'That's far more important than waiting for you and Owen to be present—there are the two dogs, you see, and he can't make up his mind which one is the better.'

'You choose,' Lallie advised, 'otherwise he'll be dithering right up till the last moment.' She became serious. 'He needs somebody like you, Vi, somebody to look after the sheep while he trains dogs.'

'The fact hadn't escaped me,' Vi said ruefully. 'It's a good job I like sheep!' She became businesslike. 'Now, shall we get on,' she murmured. 'I know a bride's allowed a little latitude in the matter of time, but not all that much.'

'Owen might run away?' Lallie laughed. She had

only said it, she hadn't meant it. The chances of Owen running away were nil. He'd made up his mind and he'd wait till Domesday, but at least one good thing had come out of this ghastly mess—Jonty and Vi. No, two! as she remembered Dwynwen.

Vi twitched the last fold of the long veil into place and bent to kiss Lallie's cheek. 'You look wonderful, that dress is just right, so simple, the princess line suits you—you're too small for frills.'

'Just what I thought,' Lallie grinned. 'I saw a beauty, but then I thought of it on me and went cold. I'd have looked like the fairy on top of the Christmas tree, but I'm afraid I shan't get voted bride of the year, I don't have any bridesmaids, and they're a must for a truly good wedding.' She grimaced. 'I only hope they don't stick to the strict etiquette all the way through, though, because if they do that, the church is going to keel over on one side with the weight of Owen's relations. I haven't any of my own.'

'Cheer up,' Vi chuckled. 'As from about half past eleven, you'll have all of Owen's, and that includes me! Shall you like that, do you think?'

'I'll love it, a real family at last, but I'll have to be careful, I've got a sharp tongue.'

'Marriage might cure it,' Vi said serenely.

Not marriage, Lallie thought. Owen would cure it or make it worse!

She supposed it was a nice wedding, although, looking back on it, she didn't remember very much. There was Jonty's arm firm beneath her hand as they walked down the aisle; it comforted her until she caught sight of Owen's russet brown head slicked down to a dark red. He really did look very good in thin suiting, just as good as he looked in tweeds, and he turned his head to watch her come. From this distance and through the corner of veil over her face, he looked quite pleasant, not in the least as though he was beginning the 'punishment of Lallie'.

She heard the murmur of responses and was surprised to discover her voice was quite steady. It didn't squeak or hesitate, but the words meant nothing to her, they were just words she was repeating after somebody else, like a child in school.

She hadn't wanted to 'obey', but as Owen had pointed out, that was part of the bargain, and when he kissed her—it was a proper kiss, not the usual peck on the cheek—she met his mouth with her own as though she was frozen all the way through.

She remembered the Community Centre, the only hall in Trellwyd big enough to hold the Tudors and the rest of the relatives. Caterers had arranged long tables and there seemed to be a lot to drink, she spied a couple of cases of champagne, and then there were the speeches. Owen's best man, a colleague from the Trellwyd practice, was very witty, although he made one or two bawdy jokes which would have better been kept for the Rugby Club of which he was an ardent member.

And there were the photographers and a host of people she didn't know and had never met, but she smiled. Oh yes, she smiled. Oh yes, she smiled until she thought her face would crack, all the time conscious of Owen sitting next to her at the top table. She didn't want anything to eat, but she gulped a glass of wine thirstily and followed it with two glasses of champagne. Somebody in London had once told her that the world always looked rosier through the bottom of a wine glass.

The wine warmed her and the champagne bubbles exploded and fizzed in her veins. When people came to wish her well, she discovered she could smile real smiles at them, even venture a little joke, so she had another glass of the stuff; the world was looking rosier already!

'How much?' That was Owen being censorious as they were driven back to Bryn Celyn ahead of the closer relatives and the friends who had been invited.

'One glass of wine and three of champagne,' Lallie said sedately. 'I feel better already.'

'On an empty stomach!' He snorted. 'You'll be lucky if you aren't sick!'

'There you go again,' she sighed, 'getting at me. It's your favourite hobby, I think. Why don't you start a "let's put Lallie down" club? This is the first time today when I've felt anywhere near happy, and you have to go and spoil it all!'

The hire car stopped in the farmyard and she scrambled out without waiting for the door to be opened, to run up the garden path as fast as her long skirts and thin satin high-heeled shoes would allow, arriving at the door hot and breathless. Once inside, she gathered up her skirts and took the stairs at a run, and in her bedroom she tore off the hampering veil, threw her bouquet across the room, kicked off her shoes and wriggled desperately to unfasten the zip of her dress.

'Damn,' she swore aloud, crying with vexation. 'Damn, damn, *damn*!'

'Allow me.' Owen was behind her and under his hands the zip ran smoothly down. He then walked across to the window and retrieved the flowers from where she had hurled them. 'You save these,' he said sternly. 'You put them on your mother's grave, that's the custom.'

'Sorry.' She slumped on the bed in her slip. 'It's been a bit much. All this fuss for a farce!'

Without a word, he lifted her feet and put them on the bed, arranging the eiderdown over her. 'Go to sleep, Lallie, you'll feel better when you wake up.'

She glared at him from the pillow. 'I'll never feel better, never!'

'Yes, you will,' he was emphatic. 'A couple of days and you . . .'

'I won't know what I was fussing about,' she finished it for him. 'You've shortened the time limit, haven't you? The last time you said that, it was a year, if I remember rightly.'

'A year, a day, what does it matter?' He pushed her back on to the pillows. 'Have a nap for an hour and I'll wake you with a cup of tea and something to eat.'

'But I can't stay up here for an hour,' she protested. 'What will everybody think?'

'What they like.' Owen was unmoved. 'I'll tell them you're changing, and everyone knows how long that takes.' And he was gone, the door closing behind him softly.

Lallie turned her face into the pillows, closing her eyes on the tears that were filling them. An hour, that was time enough to have a good old-fashioned cry, but she didn't. Her eyes closed and she drifted off to sleep.

Owen was a good timekeeper, he shook her shoulder exactly one hour later with a plate of ham sandwiches and a large mug of well sweetened tea.

'Eat them, girl,' he nodded at the plate, 'and keep your mouth busy. I want to talk to you.'

'Talk away.' Lallie had regained a little of her self-confidence, she now thought she could face about anything that came her way. She gulped thirstily at the tea and bit into a sandwich. 'Tell all,' she said with her mouth full.

'We were going away.'

'Mmm,' she nodded. 'A great secret, one I wasn't to know anything about. What was the destination, Devil's Island?' She crammed the last of the sandwich into her mouth and reached for another one. 'Oh, I forgot, there's an egg in one of my shoes in the wardrobe. Will you take it down when you go, throw it away or put it in the pigswill?'

'An egg?' He raised his eyebrows. 'What have you been playing at?'

'It was my breakfast, but I couldn't eat it,' she explained, 'and I didn't want to hurt Nerys's feelings. I thought she would be pleased with an empty tray, especially as she came up here this morning just to bring it to me. A bit mad on my part, though, I forgot about the shell, she'd expect to see that.' She stopped, looking at him. 'You said we *were* going away?'

'But not now,' he nodded. 'I'm sorry, Lallie, but I had a phone call from Jeff, Dorcas's husband, just before I left for the church. I phoned right away and cancelled our bookings.'

'What's wrong?' She felt herself going cold. 'Is Dorcas all right?'

'She went into hospital this morning—an emergency,' he explained. 'They're trying to save the baby, and Dorcas isn't in a very good condition either.'

'Then why on earth did you go on with this foolishness?' she demanded. 'We'll have to leave straight away for Cardiff—just give me ten minutes and I'll be ready . . .'

'Not yet.' He put a hand on her shoulder to push her back on the bed. 'Jeff's ringing as soon as there's any news and we can make it in an hour and a half if we have to.'

Fear trickled down her spine. 'Have you told Dwynny?'

'No,' he shook his head. 'She's coming on so well, I don't like to take the chance of upsetting her unnecessarily. Time enough for her to know if anything goes wrong. Meanwhile, will you stay up here . . .'

'But . . .'

'We've already left, my little bride. We went off quietly about a quarter of an hour ago, without anybody seeing us. The bride was a bit embarrassed and she didn't want any more fuss, she objects to confetti. If we have to go, I'd like you to go over to Jonty's with Vi.'

Instead of intense pleasure, Lallie felt chagrin. 'I'd rather come with you.'

'No.' Owen was firm and there was a hard line to his mouth which brooked no dispute. 'We have to think of the other end. Jeff's spending his time at the hospital and his mother's holding the fort. If we have to go down, Jonty and I can make do with a couch or the floor, if we have to—she knows that. If you go down, she'll feel bound to offer you something better and she has too much on her mind already without going to a lot of trouble for you. Jonty and I will go and you'll stay with Vi. That's settled!'

'Very well.' She was grudging about it. 'But for how long do I have to hide up here?'

Owen didn't answer, his head was cocked as he listened to footsteps coming along the passage. They stopped at the bathroom door and went in. 'You'll keep out of the way until the last of the stragglers have gone,' he spoke very quietly, a murmurous whisper which wouldn't penetrate the closed door. 'And I think you'd better not stay here after all— somebody else is bound to use the bathroom. Get yourself a change of clothes and as soon as the coast is clear, I'll take you where you'll be safe.'

She put out a tentative hand to cover his. 'I'm sorry, Owen. You've been worried about Dorcas and I've been behaving like a first-class bitch.'

'Oh, lord, Lallie, do you realise what you've done? You've made me an apology, about the first ever in your life!'

'Treasure it,' she advised sardonically. 'It may be the one and only. I'm not given to many moments of weakness.'

CHAPTER TEN

WHILE Owen's back was turned, Lallie wriggled out of the long white slip and replaced it with one of daytime length. She also kicked off the white satin shoes and stuffed her feet into a pair of black pumps. He gave her no time for anything more, turning to toss a cotton kimono at her and catch up her case which was standing by the bed, already packed.

'Come *on!*' he said softly as she pushed her arms into the wide cotton sleeves. 'The coast is clear.' And she found herself swept out, along the passage, past the top of the stairs and into the old wing of the house. Owen threw open the door to the room into which he had moved when Stella came to stay.

'Do you think you can be happy here?'

Lallie looked around. She knew the room, of course, but it was only a casual knowing, she had only ever been in it three or four times and never after her mother had died. It was big, occupying all the top floor of the gable end, and there was plenty of space. There were a couple of chintz-covered wing armchairs and a small table under the wide window, but these pieces of furniture didn't crowd the large bed and the rest of the massive bedroom furniture.

She walked across floorboards uneven with age and sat in one of the chairs. 'Does it matter,' she enquired bleakly, 'whether I'm happy or not? Surely it's a matter of adjustment, getting used to something different. I've discovered that everything becomes tolerable, given time.' She shivered slightly; the tiny diamond-shaped panes of the window seemed to cut out a lot of the warmth from the spring sunshine.

'At least it's big,' she murmured with a sideways glance at the very large bed. 'We shan't be cramped for space.'

'I want it this way.' Owen bent to put a match to the ready-laid fire, 'and you want it this way as well; so why can't you be honest about it? You'll be happy.'

'But it's all been so unnecessary,' she sighed mournfully. 'You've jumped the gun. Dwynny's better, Stella's gone and now Vi tells me that she and Jonty are getting married. There's no point in all this, no point at all. Why can't you be satisfied with arranging things for everybody else and leave me alone? As for being happy, what's that but saying the things you *want* to hear and believe?'

'You'd find it a relief . . .' He came towards her, very big under the low, raftered ceiling—almost menacing.

'Here we go again!' she gave an exasperated snort. 'Confess your wicked doings, Lallie—your falls from grace. Spit it all out and Owen will magnanimously forgive you your trespasses. He won't throw it in your face more than once every five minutes—but never mind that. Comfort yourself with the thought you've told all.' Her tone changed and became defiant. 'I told you the truth, if you don't want to believe my first story, believe the second. It's no skin off my nose.'

'You used to be an honest little thing,' he reminded her. 'You always owned up when you were to blame . . .'

'. . . So, I've changed.' Courage was seeping back into her, stiffening her backbone and making her waspish. 'And I won't take this "holier than thou" attitude, not from you, Owen. I wouldn't mind so much if you'd been particularly virtuous, but you haven't. The pot calling the kettle black! Don't you dare to criticise anything I've done!'

'But I've been honest about it,' he reminded her.

'So was I,' she snorted, 'and where did it get me? Go away, and since I have to hide up here because of that honesty of yours, see if you can find me something more to eat. I'm still starving.' The fire had caught well and she dragged her chair across to it. 'If you'll kindly go, I'll get dressed, it's a bit chilly sitting here in a robe.' She kicked off her shoes and held her feet out to the blaze. 'You'll let me know if you hear anything from Dorcas, won't you?'

'Of course.' Owen made no attempt to leave. 'But you and Dorcas, you were never close, were you?'

'No, not very.' Lallie wave a deprecatory hand. 'My fault, I suppose—at least, that's what you'll say, but she was always so good, so easy, and not a prickle in sight.' She stared at the flames. 'I used to envy her, though—she really belonged, I was just a stray.'

'A bit more self-pity!' He raised an eyebrow. 'You were both treated alike by all of us, weren't you? And after our parents were killed, if you found any difference in that treatment, it was because it was long overdue. You'd been allowed far too much of your own way!'

'Oooh!' Lallie clenched her hands until her nails bit into the flesh. 'What a nice way of saying I was spoiled rotten! That's what you said before, and coming from you, I prefer it,' and she glared savagely at the door as it closed behind him.

Ten minutes later, she was dressed in a grey skirt and a pink jumper, but she was still shivering. It had nothing to do with the temperature, the room was warm—it was sheer nerves, a nasty sick feeling in the pit of her stomach that wouldn't go away, not even when Vi tapped and came in with a tray, her mouth stretched in a wide smile.

'At last I've met Dwynwen. Formidable, isn't she?—reminds me of my gran.'

Lallie huddled back in her chair and stretched cold fingers to the fire. 'How did it go?'

'Much as I expected,' Vi chuckled. 'A stern lecture on the errors of my ways and then an abrupt volte-face because we *are* getting married, which will put everything right, and she's decided that Jonty was probably as much to blame as me. It takes two to tango, although she didn't quite put it that way.'

'She barks a lot,' Lallie murmured, her eyes fixed on the tray. 'But there's not much bite to it. It's her chapel morality warring with her devotion to the family. Now you're going to be a Tudor, you're above reproach. Is that soup?'

'Mmm; and some more ham sandwiches. I'm sorry it isn't anything more exciting, but Jonty's only just managed to get rid of the stragglers, two distant cousins, I believe, who've been inspecting the wedding presents. He's just driven them back to Trell-wyd. I do think he's improving, he did it alone and unaided—no mean feat, I might add, they looked as though they'd taken root in the parlour. Do you want me to stay with you for a while?'

'I'll be glad of the company.' Lallie glanced at her watch. 'Oh dear, it's only half past seven—it seems like a lifetime since this morning. There's no news about Dorcas yet?'

'Not yet.' Vi dragged the other chair across to the fire. 'There are some things that can't be rushed, you know, although human beings aren't as bad as sheep. Ewes can put it off for ages if they're disturbed.'

'Sensible creatures.' Lallie drank her soup and started on a sandwich, but her appetite had gone, lost in nervousness, and she started to shiver again. Vi looked at her compassionately.

'Hinny, you're out on your feet—don't bother about that sandwich, go and lie down for a while. When I get married, it's going to be as quick and simple as possible, this long-drawn-out business is far too traumatic. I'd never stand it.'

'What will you wear?'

'This, I think.' Vi gestured at her bronze silk. 'Quite suitable, don't you think, and I'll have an orchid spray to make it look festive. Come on now,' she took the remains of the sandwich from Lallie's unresisting fingers, tossed it on the tray and urged her towards the bed, 'strip off and have a rest.'

'I've only just dressed!' Lallie fought off inactivity.

'Then undress,' Vi said firmly. 'Have a nap, and when you wake, there may be some news. You'll be able to come downstairs and we'll eat properly, something hot.'

Lallie allowed herself to be persuaded, stripping once more down to her underwear and sliding beneath the eiderdown. 'Go back downstairs,' she muttered. 'Jonty'll be back soon and he'll be missing you.' She smothered a yawn of mammoth proportions, her eyes closed and although she thought she would never be able to, she slept.

It seemed only minutes later that she was awakened as Owen dropped his large frame on to the edge of the bed. She blinked at him, at the unfamiliar room, while she orientated herself. The window was quite dark now and the fire had died to a dull glow which barely illuminated his face. He put out a hand and switched on the bedside lamp, and she looked at him speculatively, with new eyes, wondering if any other newly-wedded wife felt as she felt—nervous but somehow not afraid, either of him or of the future.

She had been dragooned into marriage—no, that wasn't correct. If the idea of it had been that distasteful to her, nothing, but nothing, would have made her marry him—she wasn't the stuff of which martyrs were made. It was very nice, very propitiating to think of herself as being pushed around against her will, but it was a long way from the truth. If she hadn't wanted to be pushed around, she could have thought of some other way out of the mess.

Owen kept on and on about honesty; she tried to be honest. The truth was, it was a mess she wanted to be in, a nice mess, a lovely mess, and she would enjoy as much of it as she could. There would be bad patches, but she thought she could cope with them. A little frisson of excitement made her shiver.

'Something going round in that clever little brain of yours, Lallie?' Owen sounded amused.

'Some,' she admitted, and then, 'Have you heard from Dorcas?'

'Mmm, five minutes ago. A boy, caesarian section, rather small and a bit frail, which was to be expected—he's come very early into the world, and Dorcas isn't all that bright and sparkling, but they're both out of danger.'

'Oh.' The tension in her released as though a spring which had been wound too tightly had been slackened off. 'Then it's all right, you won't have to go down to Cardiff.'

'No, Jonty's taken Vi home and the only place I'm going is to bed.' Owen lifted a corner of the eiderdown and examined her semi-clothed state. 'You're surely not intending to sleep like that, Lallie?' He inserted a long finger under the clip of her bra. 'You'll find it very uncomfortable.' He tipped up the lid of her case and examined the contents, grimacing at the two printed cotton nighties she had packed.

'Not glamorous,' he murmured, 'or very seductive. Is this the best you could do, or don't you think I'm worth anything better?'

Without waiting for a reply, he put the contents of his pockets on to the bedside table, discarded his jacket and stripped off his tie. 'There's a bathroom just down the passage, I'll use the other one for tonight. Be back in about ten minutes.'

Owen was being calm and matter-of-fact; it chilled her, but it effectively steadied her nerves. If he could treat this as an ordinary, everyday happening, so could she, so that when he returned to the bedroom she was standing by the darkened window, apparently calm.

'Lallie.' She looked back across the room, blinking as her eyes adjusted to the light, and her heart gave a leap in her breast at the sight of him in a short towelling robe and with the russet of his hair slicked back to darkness with water.

'Yes?' She had meant her voice to be calm, unruffled, but it came out as a gasp.

'Come to bed, Lallie,' and quietly, she allowed him to take her hand and lead her away from the window, back to the dying glow of the fire. 'I don't like it,' he gestured at the cotton nightie. 'How does it come off?'

'Over my head, usually.' She heard herself sounding rather breathless. 'I'm afraid what's underneath it isn't all that glamorous either.' Her small laugh had an almost hysterical quality. 'Unlike your previous girl-friends, I have a little less, not more,' and as his fingers slipped buttons and he pushed the garment from her shoulders to drop at her feet, 'I told you I was f-flat-chested!'

She would have said more, but his mouth was on hers and this didn't seem to be the moment for talking. She wished she could plead with him to be gentle, but his mouth was a hot, demanding pressure and her own hunger broke loose under it. She struggled her arms up about his neck, clinging tightly to him while her fingers threaded through his thick hair, and as her lips trembled and parted under his, she felt herself picked up and carried to the bed, to sheets which were a cool linen against her feverish body.

Between kisses that grew steadily more hungry, she heard Owen murmuring, but the words were just words that didn't matter any more. They were sounds, comforting noises, and she struggled closer to him, trembling violently as his hands caressed her. She had a feeling of exhilarating freedom which seemed to come from them being so close together, and her slender body arched to meet his with a breathless uncertainty that vanished in an explosion of joy so wild and primitive she thought she would die of it.

Lallie opened her eyes to a grey half-light, her hand moving to seek the warmth of Owen's, to feel again the silk of his skin against hers, but she was alone. In all the width of the bed, there was nothing of him, not even the warmth where he'd been. She dragged herself upright, clutching the covers about her bare shoulders to keep out the chill of the early morning. He'd gone—he'd been disappointed—she'd been clumsy—untutored . . . and then the bedroom door opened and he was with her, sitting on the side of the bed and proffering tea.

He watched in silence as she drank it, his face a hard, angry mask.

'So you didn't!' He took the empty cup from her fingers and put it on the floor. She was grateful for the few seconds' respite, it gave her time to pull herself together. The wild sweetness of the night was gone and this was another day when life, cold and practical, was attacking her, and she fought back.

'I told you I didn't, but you wouldn't believe me,'

she scolded. 'You were raging with temper then, and now you know I didn't, you're still raging. What's with you, Owen—some hang-up about despoiling virgins?'

'You didn't act like one,' he pointed out.

'There's a way to act?' She raised a derisive eyebrow.

'Stop it, Lallie—don't you understand? I would have been more gentle—I could have hurt you. Did I?'

Her shrug was eloquent. 'Does it matter? But that's not what's making you savage.'

'No.' His face grew harder, his brows a frowning line above his masterful nose. 'It's the thought of that damned old man and what he did to you, putting you through hell . . .'

'Forget it.' She was brief and as cold and hard as he. 'I never blamed him. He had his reasons and to him they were good—a theatre, a play in which he'd sunk about every penny he possessed and a cast which was depending on him for their wages. Compared to all that, what's the reputation of an unknown little typist? I *told* you, it was a publicity stunt. We'd been working late at rehearsals and he wanted the rewritten script for the next morning—he'd even hired a copier. He took me back to his house, we finished off the work well after midnight and he offered me a bed, that was all. I think he was rather ashamed of himself, knowing what was going to happen. No, the people I blamed were those who believed the filth that was published, not so much the ordinary men and women, they didn't know me from Adam. That's when you hurt me, Owen. Not last night, but then! When, knowing me since I was four years old, you believed it of me even when I denied it over and over again. Maybe I think you wanted to believe it.'

'Don't be a little fool, Lallie.' Unconcernedly he stripped off the towelling robe and slid into bed beside her, one heavy arm and a muscular leg pinning her wriggling body down firmly. 'For ten years I've been after you, my girl, and while I admit that, like any other man, I'd prefer to be first with my wife, I could live with it if I wasn't.'

'T-ten years!' she squeaked. 'Are you having me on, Owen? You've always disapproved of me . . .'

'Stupid!' His free hand tangled with her rope of hair, grasped it firmly and held her head still while, leisurely and with evident enjoyment, he kissed her trembling mouth. 'I love you, my silly little darling, I always have.'

'You love me? That's something you say, and I don't believe it. Nobody who loved me could treat me as you've done.'

'Ever since you were a kid,' he assured her, 'and I wanted you when you were sixteen, even before that, but you were too young. Dwynwen knew about it and she warned me off. You had to be given time, she said—no good would come of rushing things—so I backed off and cracked down on you hard. You needed it, you tempestuous little witch—you were becoming the next best thing to a delinquent.'

'I was not!' She tried to work herself up into a rage, but he interrupted.

'. . . Be quiet while I have my say. Things started to go wrong almost as soon as I'd decided to give you a bit of growing room. Jonty said he wanted to marry you, he was all set to ask you, so I fobbed him off with Dwynwen's story and schemed a bit to get you out of his way. The scheming paid off and you went to London. Neat, wasn't it?'

'Oh, very.' Lallie wriggled and then lay still. 'Operation performed successfully and the scar hardly shows now. You're a dab hand with a surgeon's knife, Owen—you cut me adrift. . .'

'And then, before Jonty had time to get over it properly, you landed yourself in trouble in London. He was all set to come down, galloping to your rescue like a modern Galahad. He'd marry you, he said, and bring you back here. I couldn't let that happen, *cariad* . . .'

'I wasn't good enough for Jonty, is that what you mean?'

'You haven't been listening.' Owen pulled her more closely against him. 'It wasn't that and you know it. I couldn't have you here, not married to Jonty—you might have accepted him as a way out, and I couldn't take a chance on that happening. You and he together here, married—I wouldn't have slept until I'd taken you away from him, and a nice scandal that would have been! Me and my brother's wife . . .'

'You're very sure of yourself!' she tried to sneer, but it didn't come out that way. Her chin wobbled and her eyes filled with tears. 'As if I would ever have let you do a thing like that to Jonty! Never, not in a million years!'

'Of course you wouldn't,' he murmured into her neck. 'You'd have taken off for parts unknown and we'd both have lost you. I had to think of another way, so I came down to London myself.'

'And you wouldn't believe me . . .'

'Whether I believed you or not was immaterial, but I couldn't bring you back here. Jonty was too vulnerable,' Owen's smile was wry. 'So was I, *anwylyd*! You'd have had us at each other's throats in no time flat. You *had* to stay away until he got over you. That's why I forbade you to come here.'

'How nice!' She refused to be mollified. 'I had to sweat it out in London while you, you bastard, held Jonty's hand, bolstered his ego and told him to write me off like a bad debt. How like you, Owen!'

'But you were always a strong character, Lallie, and you know Jonty isn't. He needs a prop, he did then, and he still needs one. Vi may not realise, but that's what she will be—somebody for him to rely on, to cling to, somebody who'll take care of him, organise his life and his work—put him back on the rails every time he falls off.' His lips trailed from her throat to her cheek and then across to each eyelid in turn. 'But you, my darling, I knew you'd manage. It would take more than a bit of bad publicity to get you down.'

'It nearly did,' she muttered.

'Nonsense,' he chuckled. 'You're a fighter, my girl, you'd not give up while you had breath left in you. I'm only sorry it took so long.'

'Six years!' she accused. 'That's a hell of a long time to leave a girl to get on by herself!'

'Well, I had to wait for the right opportunity, didn't I?' Owen was seriously reasonable. 'If I'd come for you without a good reason, you'd have scratched my eyes out. You were hating me, my love, I was the wicked fairy. In any case, you left the place where I'd left you in safety and you'd left the job I found for you. You disappeared, and it wasn't until old Tommy Griffiths wrote for a character reference that I knew where you were working. It took a long time and a lot of guile to find out where you lived. Dwynwen wouldn't give me your address.'

'I could have married somebody else, somebody in London.' Lallie was still defiant. 'I've had offers.'

'And I've said, I'd have taken you away from Jonty, and that goes for any other man you married . . .'

'You wouldn't,' she flared. 'You couldn't!'

'I would and I could.' Owen's arm tightened about her. 'I'm being honest, *cariad*. We're two of a kind, we belong together. You tried your road and it wasn't any good, was it? You'll like mine much better, that's why I've dragged you down it with me.'

'Your road?' She raised brimming eyes to his face and gulped at a sob. 'It doesn't look all that wonderful to me, not what I've seen of it so far. All I have to do is say "Please", "Thank you" and "May I?" It's not a road, it's penal servitude!'

'Precisely, my little love, and it goes on to Forever—but tell me, which one of us, do you think, is in chains?'

'I am . . . I'm bogged down with them!'

'Liar!' His hand slid from her waist to her hips in a caressing movement and pulled her closer to him. 'We both are, wench. You to me and me to you. If you run out on me, I'll follow. I'll bring you back and you'll come, because neither of us has any option. We're part of each other, this is where we belong, and we belong together.'

'And you call that love! It doesn't sound very comfortable to me.' She screwed up her nose. 'When do we get to the rack and thumbscrew thing?'

'Stop it, *cariad*,' and she felt the rumble of laughter in his chest. 'You don't have to be clever with me any longer. The war's over, we made peace last night—and don't try to tell me that wasn't satisfactory.'

'I'm not quite convinced yet,' she murmured. 'I've this feeling I've been pressured into it. You seem to have had it all worked out while I was in the dark and playing it by ear. Why didn't you tell me about loving me before?'

'And have you spit in my eye?' There was a long pause, and after he had reluctantly raised his mouth from hers, 'You'd have been so bloody triumphant, you'd have kept me on my knees for months!'

'That'll be the day,' she said darkly. 'When you go down on your knees, I'd like to see it. One thing, though, there aren't going to be any more weekend "conferences", so you can put them out of your mind straight away!'

Owen chuckled. 'Conferences are always at weekends, my pet, and attendance is nearly compulsory. How else do you think vets keep up with modern methods?'

'Huh!' she snorted disbelievingly. 'You forget, I know you, Owen. We used to have bets on which girl you were taking when I was at school. We all used to put tenpence in the kitty and the one who guessed right scooped the pool. I only won it once, and then they wouldn't let me take my winnings, they said I had access to private information.'

'Well,' he admitted grudgingly, 'there were one or two, but never as many as you all thought, and they didn't mean anything. It was just something to keep my mind off a black-haired little terror who ripped up my peace and had me walking the floor at night wondering if she'd scream blue murder if I went into her room and made love to her. Lallie,' he groaned, 'sometimes it was hell, and this last couple of months hasn't been easy either. I've been hurting with wanting you.'

'How stupid can you get?' she chuckled, holding his face between her hands and looking into his eyes where the little yellow flames were dancing. 'Oh dear,' the expression on her face was comical—half dismay, half hidden happiness. 'I hope you don't expect me to reform, because I don't think I could— my damn tongue . . .'

'But you've got such nice party manners.' His eyes slitted with laughter. 'You put them on like Sunday best clothes whenever anybody's about. Look at the way you've handled Dwynwen and how you coped with Stella. You should have tried for the Diplomatic Service and thrown your typewriter on the scrap heap. It's only with me that the cross-grained little madam shows through.'

'I had to keep my end up,' Lallie protested. 'Otherwise you'd have walked all over me. Besides,' she grinned, 'I like a good fight.'

'It depends on **who** you're fighting.' Owen's hands were gentle at her breasts as though he was telling her that this was no time for war. 'You didn't have to fight me, Lallie.'

She became serious. 'I don't think I was fighting you—I mean, more doing battle with myself for being such a weak-kneed idiot.'

'Weak?' He obviously didn't agree with her character reading of herself. 'Weak about what?'

'Loving you, Owen.' She looked into his face with wide, candid eyes. 'I didn't know about it, not at first. When I was little, I used to think you were wonderful, but then I started hating . . .'

'A defence mechanism,' he said tersely. 'But there's no need for it now. The battle's over, and we both win.'

'Mmm, but we've wasted a lot of time, haven't we?'

'There you go again,' he objected. 'Making sweeping statements. *We* haven't wasted time, *you* did that!'

Lallie sighed and pulled his head closer. 'Don't let's waste any more,' she breathed softly against his mouth. 'Oh, my darling . . . !'